Bull in a
China Shop

by G. B. Gilford

SAMUEL FRENCH

FOUNDED 1830

SAMUELFRENCH.COM

BULL IN A CHINA SHOP was originally published in ELLERY QUEEN'S MYSTERY MAGAZINE, and selected as one of the best mystery stories of the year for inclusion in the anthology BEST DETECTIVE STORIES OF 1957, published by E. P. Dutton and Company. When it was performed as one of the ALFRED HITCHCOCK PRESENTS television series, the cast featured Estelle Winwood as Hildegarde, Elizabeth Patterson as Birdie, and Dennis Morgan as O'Finn.

THE SCENE

The short scenes at the police station are played in front of the act curtain, without scenery. The main setting represents the old-fashioned parlor of 909 Sycamore Street, a boarding house for ancient females.

THE CAST
(in the order of their appearance)

DENNIS O'FINN, *Detective First Class*

MISS HILDEGARDE, *the landlady*

MISS BIRDIE

MISS AMANTHA

MISS LUCY

MISS NETTIE

MISS ELIZABETH

KRAMER, *Detective Second Class*

FIRST STRETCHER BEARER

SECOND STRETCHER BEARER

JANE ROGERS, *reporter for the Herald-Globe*

JOHNSON, *police fingerprint expert*

ABOUT THE AUTHOR

Charles Bernard Gilford is a Missourian by birth. He was educated at Rockhurst College and the Catholic University of America, and earned his doctorate in theatre at the University of Denver. After serving three years as a B-29 navigator in the Pacific area of combat, he returned to the teaching profession and has served on the faculties of Rockhurst College and Saint Louis University, where he now conducts graduate courses in theatre arts. He is widely experienced as a director and has acted professionally for television. Dr. Gilford devotes most of his spare time to writing, and has sold more than fifty stories to national magazines. He is a frequent contributor to ALFRED HITCHCOCK PRESENTS, the top mystery series, and to other network television programs. One of his stories, JOY RIDE, was recently purchased by Allied Artists Pictures Corporation. Dr. Gilford is married to the former Martha Campbell of Kansas City. They have four children.

ACT ONE

(Lights come up on the apron of the stage, with the act curtain closed. DENNIS O'FINN is revealed in the light. He is a well-built man in his forties, with a winning Irish smile and personality. He is wearing a plain business suit and hat. He speaks directly to the audience.)

O'FINN. My name is Dennis O'Finn. Ah, that's a familiar name to you, isn't it? You've seen it in the papers. Well, I'm here to tell you, it was all a pack of lies. Well now . . . maybe not all of it was lies exactly. There were a few murders. But there was a great misunderstanding about my part in it. As you can well see, I'm not nearly as handsome and charming as the newspaper stories made out. I'm just an ordinary Irish cop. O'Finn, plain-clothes detective, first class, attached to Homicide Division. And I'm forty years old, for Heaven's sake. And a bachelor besides. So I couldn't have gone on being a bachelor for forty years if I was so handsome and charming, now could I? Well now, you can see for yourself. The whole thing probably started with a scene that looked something like this. . . .

(The lights go out on the apron. In the black-out the curtain rises, and when the stage lights come up, we see an interior. It is the old-fashioned parlor of the house at 909 Sycamore Street, a boarding house for ancient females. There are six of these females altogether, and they are all here at the moment, all shapes and sizes, but they have a few things in common. They are all old, lonely, and a little queer. There is MISS HILDEGARDE, the landlady of the establishment, MISS BIRDIE, MISS AMANTHA, MISS LUCY, MISS NETTIE, and MISS ELIZABETH. Note that they are all "Misses." There is a certain similarity in their apparel too. They are all wearing dresses which were in style about forty years ago, which was the time when the ladies themselves—if they ever were—were in style too. At this moment they are all clustered about the window. MISS ELIZABETH is standing on a chair, and so towers over the rest. She has a pair of binoculars, and is peering out.)

AMANTHA. Elizabeth, what's he doing now?
ELIZABETH. He's in his undershirt.
BIRDIE. Can you see the strawberry mark on his shoulder?
ELIZABETH. I certainly can. Clear as day.
AMANTHA. Oh, let me see.
NETTIE. No, Amantha, it's my turn.
BIRDIE. The binoculars belong to me, don't forget.
ELIZABETH. But your eyesight is bad, remember, Birdie dear. I can describe everything to you, can't I?
BIRDIE. But I want to see for myself.
ELIZABETH. He has such wonderfully big muscles in his arms. Do you know what he's doing now?

5

NETTIE. What? Tell us. For pity's sake, tell us.

ELIZABETH. He's doing calisthenics, that's what. And he's using dumbbells or something. They look awfully big and heavy.

NETTIE. That's what gives him the muscles.

ELIZABETH. Oh, yes, he's awfully strong. He's lifting the dumbbells and swinging them around, as if they didn't weigh anything at all.

HILDEGARDE. (*Tugging at ELIZABETH'S skirt*) Elizabeth, give me those glasses. I want to see this with my own eyes.

ELIZABETH. (*Not budging*) I'm describing it to you, aren't I?

HILDEGARDE. But I want to see.

ELIZABETH. I got here first.

BIRDIE. But they're my binoculars.

HILDEGARDE. But you're looking through my window. Because this is my house. Now give me a look or I'll . . .

AMANTHA. We should all have a turn.

LUCY. Just knock the chair out from under her feet, that's the thing to do.

BIRDIE. No, no, you might break my binoculars.

ELIZABETH. (*There's an unmaidenly scuffle around the chair, which ELIZABETH interrupts by lowering the glasses and turning to the rest of them*) It's too late. He's stopped his exercises, and he's disappeared. (*They all turn away from the window in disappointment, and disperse around the room, where they sit in glum silence. ELIZABETH climbs down from the chair. Having just communed with the Great Spectacle, she is not so glum.*) Oh, it was a grand sight though.

AMANTHA. But you were so selfish about it, Elizabeth.

ELIZABETH. Amantha my dear, in these days of a man shortage, one has to be selfish.

HILDEGARDE. Elizabeth, I should have you evicted from my house.

ELIZABETH. Come now, Hildegarde. You wouldn't evict a good paying boarder, and you know it. You need the money too badly.

HILDEGARDE. I could replace you with someone who isn't so man-crazy. Maybe a widow instead of an old maid like you.

ELIZABETH. Hildegarde, then you'd have to throw everybody out. They're all old maids here. And they're all just as man-crazy as I am.

AMANTHA. I'm not man-crazy! I have a motherly feeling toward Mr. O'Finn.

NETTIE. And I have a sisterly feeling.

BIRDIE. My feeling isn't sisterly. (*She giggles.*)

LUCY. My feeling toward Mr. O'Finn is as if he were a dear nephew of mine. In fact, I'm going to make out a will and leave him my money.

HILDEGARDE. Rubbish. You don't have any money, Lucy. You're a month behind in your rent right now.

AMANTHA. Oh, stop this wrangling.

NETTIE. (*Sweetly*) We might as well wrangle. We don't have anything else to do till tea time.

AMANTHA. Well, I say we ought to be doing something more constructive.

LUCY. Such as what, Amantha?

AMANTHA. Well, I'll confess something. I'd like to get a better look at Mr. O'Finn.

LUCY. We've sat on the porch, and watched him go in and out of his apartment, haven't we?

AMANTHA. Yes, I know, but that's still clear across the street. That isn't very close. I'd like to get . . . real close to him sometime.

BIRDIE. (*Squeals in delight*) Oh, yes, so would I. Real close to him. We don't even know for sure what color his eyes are.

NETTIE. But how are we going to get close to him?

ELIZABETH. We could go for a walk on *his* side of the street, just about the time he's due to come home. After all, we do know his schedule pretty well.

HILDEGARDE. But we don't know his schedule to the very minute. There we'd be, walking up and down in front of his apartment house. People would think we were picketing.

LUCY. And we couldn't do it every day.

NETTIE. Then the only thing left is to go visit him.

BIRDIE. (*Horrified*) Nettie, *nice* ladies do *not* go visiting gentlemen.

NETTIE. All right, you figure it out then.

HILDEGARDE. The real nice thing to happen would be for Mr. O'Finn to come visiting *us*.

BIRDIE. Oh, I'm afraid I'm going to swoon, just imagining it.

LUCY. But how can we make him come visiting us?

ELIZABETH. We could sit on the front porch, in our best clothes, and look real attractive.

AMANTHA. My dear Elizabeth, you've been sitting out on the front porch for weeks, and Mr. O'Finn hasn't even glanced at you. You even sat out there during that chilly spell, and caught your death of cold.

ELIZABETH. Well, the trouble was, you know, that I can't afford any pretty new clothes in the latest styles.

LUCY. The trouble is, Elizabeth, that *you're* not very pretty.

ELIZABETH. Lucy, how dare you!

AMANTHA. Will you hush up and listen to me? We've got to do something to *make* Mr. O'Finn come to visit us. We must remember that bachelors are naturally shy. I'm convinced he won't come here unless we *arrange* it somehow.

BIRDIE. Oh, yes, let's arrange it!

NETTIE. But how?

LUCY. If he was a plumber, we could stop up the sink.

AMANTHA. But he's not a plumber.

LUCY. Or if he was a glazier, we could break a window.

AMANTHA. But he's not a glazier. And he's not a carpenter or a painter, or an electrician. Or anything convenient. He's a detective.

BIRDIE. Well, why don't we throw away my pearl necklace, and report it stolen?

ELIZABETH. Your *imitation* pearl necklace, you mean.

AMANTHA. It doesn't make any difference anyway. Mr. O'Finn works for Homicide. That means he wouldn't come here unless somebody died.

NETTIE. Well, how can we arrange for that to happen?

7

(All six of them sit silently, staring at one another, while the curtain descends slowly. When the curtain is down, the lights on the apron come up again. O'FINN is revealed. He speaks again to the audience.)

O'FINN. Well, that's approximately how I imagine it started. I didn't have an inkling about it at first, of course. All I got was a routine report. My sidekick Kramer took it on the phone. Then he came in and told me about it. This is Kramer right here. Detective second class.

(KRAMER enters onto the apron from the wings. He is another plain-clothes detective, a little younger and smaller than O'FINN. He is only a detective second class, so he has a slightly deferential attitude toward O'FINN. He is carrying a notebook, and consults it as he speaks.)

KRAMER. Hey, O'Finn, we got a little job. Report of a death at 909 Sycamore.
O'FINN. That's my street. Must be right across . . .
KRAMER. Coincidence, huh?
O'FINN. What kind of death?
KRAMER. An old lady. Some other old lady phoned in. Wanted to speak to you, in fact. Said they knew a Detective O'Finn was in Homicide. Then when I told her you were my partner and we always worked together, she seemed satisfied. But then I asked her, wasn't it a natural death? An old lady, and all that. And then she said she wasn't sure about that.
O'FINN. Well, we'd better go out and take a look. . . .

(Lights go out on the apron. The curtain rises in darkness, and then the lights go up again on the stage, at 909 Sycamore. Five of the old ladies are intact, but the sixth, MISS ELIZABETH, lies dead on the sofa. She is arranged somewhat like a corpse in a coffin, except that her get-up is gay, not somber. She is wearing MISS LUCY'S flowery hat, MISS BIRDIE'S pearl necklace, MISS NETTIE'S feather boa, and carrying MISS AMANTHA'S beaded bag. The five ladies stand around the corpse admiringly.)

AMANTHA. I think that just about does it. Doesn't she look pretty?
HILDEGARDE. I must admit it was very generous of all of you to give her your best things to wear.
NETTIE. Well, she deserves it, doesn't she? After all, if it wasn't for her, we wouldn't be getting this chance of meeting Mr. O'Finn.
LUCY. And besides, it's her *last* chance of meeting Mr. O'Finn.
BIRDIE. So she ought to look her best, I agree. That's why I sacrificed my precious pearls.
LUCY. And my hat is really becoming on her. She used to try to steal it to wear on Sundays, you know. But I forgive her now.
NETTIE. But don't you think my feather boa looks the prettiest of all? I don't know what I'll do without it. They'll bury her in it, I suppose.
AMANTHA. Yes, I'm afraid they will. That's why I took my money out of the beaded bag I gave her. She won't need money any more.

BIRDIE. Oh dear, all those pretty things gone to waste. No . . . no
. . . I didn't mean that. Elizabeth must look proper. This is the biggest
moment of her life.
(*The doorbell rings.*)
NETTIE. Oh, that's him! It must be him!
BIRDIE. I'm going to swoon. I know I'm going to swoon.
AMANTHA. You mustn't do that, Birdie. This is Elizabeth's big mo-
ment, not yours.
HILDEGARDE. Now everybody line up nice and orderly. We can't
have Mr. O'Finn think he's visiting a houseful of magpies. Everybody
behave themselves. We simply must make a good impression.

(*They line up in a sort of reception line, with ELIZABETH on the
sofa as the last one in the line. The line bends, as it were, when it gets
to ELIZABETH, however, so that anyone proceeding down this line
would not notice ELIZABETH right at first. HILDEGARDE goes to
the door and opens it. O'FINN and KRAMER step inside.*)

O'FINN. This is the house where a lady has just died?
HILDEGARDE. Yes, this is the house. I'm the one who called. I'm
Miss Hildegarde Hodge. This is my house.
O'FINN. Well, my name is O'Finn. And this is my partner, Kramer.
Now where's the body?
HILDEGARDE. First, you must meet my guests.
O'FINN. Guests?
HILDEGARDE. My permanent guests. They live here, you see. Now
this is Miss Nettie.

(*O'FINN and KRAMER begin to go down the line. Nobody pays any
attention to KRAMER. But each lady in turn grasps O'FINN'S hand
possessively and is loath to let go. He is so confused that he submits to
their scrutiny.*)

NETTIE. Oh, he does have big muscles. I can feel it the way he's hold-
ing my hand.
AMANTHA. Hush, Nettie. And it's time to let go of his hand any-
way. It's my turn.
NETTIE. Oh, all right. How are you, Mr. O'Finn?
O'FINN. Well, I'm fine. But I came here to see . . .
NETTIE. This is Miss Amantha.
O'FINN. (*In a submissive daze now*) Miss Amantha . . .
AMANTHA. Oh, you dear boy. You look a little run-down to me.
Have you been eating the right things?
O'FINN. I beg your pardon . . .
AMANTHA. Bachelors very seldom have a balanced diet, cooking for
themselves and eating out.
LUCY. (*Sharply*) Amantha!
AMANTHA. Oh, yes. Mr. O'Finn, this is Miss Lucy.
O'FINN. How do you do, Miss Lucy?

LUCY. (*After a long, soulful, mournful stare*) You remind me of Herbert.

O'FINN. Who?

LUCY. He was a young fellow I knew. But he's dead now.

O'FINN. I'm very sorry.

LUCY. Oh, that's all right. I've gotten over it.

O'FINN. Well, I'm glad to hear that.

LUCY. It was forty years ago.

BIRDIE. Lucy, I would like to be introduced to Mr. O'Finn.

LUCY. Oh, yes. Mr. O'Finn, this is Miss Birdie.

O'FINN. How do you do, Miss Birdie? What's the matter? What's wrong?

BIRDIE. I feel like swooning.

O'FINN. Well, somebody get a glass of water or something . . .

BIRDIE. Oh, don't worry. I'm not going to. Amantha said I mustn't. Not right at first anyway. She said it wouldn't be fair to Elizabeth. So maybe later, Mr. O'Finn. Will you catch me if I do?

O'FINN. I guess so. . . .

BIRDIE. That's a promise then. And don't you forget it. Now, this is Miss Elizabeth.

(*O'FINN sees the corpse for the first time. He snaps out of his daze. He and KRAMER both cross to the corpse, and take a long look.*)

KRAMER. O'Finn, are you sure she's dead? She kind of looks like she's asleep. Kind of smiling . . .

BIRDIE. Oh, she's dead all right. We wouldn't have given her all those pretty things to wear if she were alive. She was kind of mean and nasty sometimes when she was alive.

(*O'FINN bends over, takes the corpse's pulse. There is a silence.*)

NETTIE. Isn't this exciting? Too bad Elizabeth has to miss it.

LUCY. Maybe she's not really so very far away. She's not missing it unless she has to.

O'FINN. (*Stands up*) I'd say she's dead all right. No pulse. And she's cold.

BIRDIE. Oh, yes, I noticed that when I put the pearls around her neck.

O'FINN. When you what?

AMANTHA. We all dressed her up. That's why she looks so pretty. We wanted her to look her best for the occasion.

KRAMER. What occasion?

NETTIE. Receiving gentlemen, of course.

KRAMER. (*Looking helplessly at O'FINN*) Of course . . . sure . . .

O'FINN. (*Assuming command*) Okay now. Let's all sit down and talk this over. (*Most of them accept his invitation.*) Kramer, get on the phone and get the wheels working. There is a phone, isn't there?

HILDEGARDE. It's out in the kitchen.

(*KRAMER exits to the kitchen.*)

O'FINN. Now, what I'd like to know first of all is this. Miss . . .

HILDEGARDE. Hildegarde. You may use my first name.

O'FINN. Thank you. Now, Miss Hildegarde, whatever gave you the idea you ought to phone the police about this matter?

HILDEGARDE. (*Pauses and consults the other ladies with silent glances*) Because Elizabeth died under suspicious circumstances.

(*KRAMER re-enters and nods knowingly to O'FINN.*)

O'FINN. Just what was suspicious?

HILDEGARDE. It was so sudden. Dear Elizabeth was in the best of health. Then at lunch time she began acting queer.

AMANTHA. She turned kind of pale. Looked like she was getting sick.

HILDEGARDE. And then suddenly she complained of cramps.

LUCY. And then she just keeled over.

O'FINN. Did you call a doctor? (*Nobody answers. He notices the secret glances passing among them.*) Did anybody call a doctor?

AMANTHA. No, we didn't.

O'FINN. (*Amazed*) But surely you must have seen the lady was in a serious condition.

NETTIE. Well, we talked about calling a doctor.

O'FINN. You talked about it!

NETTIE. But then we decided it wasn't any use. Poor Elizabeth was already too far gone. We wanted to let her die in peace.

LUCY. You see, Mr. O'Finn, we sort of knew . . .

O'FINN. You sort of knew what?

LUCY. (*After much hesitation*) That it wasn't any use calling a doctor. Elizabeth had been poisoned.

O'FINN. (*To all of them*) Did you all think this lady had been poisoned? (*A chorus of solemn nods.*) Why did you all think she'd been poisoned? (*No reply, only cat-who-swallowed-the-canary glances among the ladies.*) Look, I asked a question, and I want an answer. Why do you think she was poisoned?

BIRDIE. (*To the other ladies*) Isn't he masterful?

LUCY. He has a strong voice just like Herbert's. Whenever Herbert shouted at me like that, it sent chills up and down my spine. I haven't had chills for forty years.

BIRDIE. Do you have chills now?

LUCY. I certainly do.

O'FINN. Now see here. You ladies don't seem to realize how important . . . I'm a police officer, and I'm here to investigate a homicide. And it's just been suggested that this lady was poisoned. Now I want to know more about that!

HILDEGARDE. (*Chidingly*) Mr. O'Finn, you are raising your voice unnecessarily. Perhaps you have misjudged our ages. None of us is deaf.

KRAMER. (*Beginning to enjoy the situation and O'FINN'S frustration, he mocks his partner*) Oh, yes, Mr. O'Finn, watch yourself. And none of your station house language here, either. There are ladies present.

O'FINN. (*Wrathful*) All right, Kramer, if you're so smart. You ask the questions. See if you can get any answers.

KRAMER. Don't look at me. You're the boss.

BIRDIE. That's right, Mr. O'Finn. And we won't answer any questions unless they come from the *boss*.

O'FINN. Well, somebody answer my question then.

HILDEGARDE. What do you think, Mr. O'Finn? You're the detective. Do you think she was poisoned?

O'FINN. My dear lady . . .

HILDEGARDE. (*Interrupting, to the other ladies*) Did you hear that? He called me his dear lady.

O'FINN. (*Trying to ignore these sallies*) We will not know whether poison caused the death until there's an examination of the body. It will take a doctor to do that. But now I think there'd better be an examination.

NETTIE. Oh, but we already know.

O'FINN. (*Pouncing*) Why do you know?

NETTIE. Somebody had to die.

HILDEGARDE. Nettie, please. Let Mr. O'Finn find out for himself. It won't be any fun if we tell him everything.

O'FINN. (*Exploding*) What is all this? You all know the lady was poisoned. You seem to know a lot more than that, in fact. Like *how* she was poisoned, for instance. Well, somebody had better talk.

BIRDIE. You mean a third degree?

NETTIE. With bright lights in our eyes?

LUCY. I'm first.

HILDEGARDE. Why should you be first?

LUCY. (*Darkly*) Because I know more about the people in this house than anybody else. And I could tell Mr. O'Finn a thing or two about everybody.

AMANTHA. It'll be lies. All lies. You never tell the truth, Lucy.

O'FINN. Stop it! Stop it! (*He takes KRAMER aside and they talk in low tones so the ladies can't hear.*) This place is a booby hatch. I've got to get out of here.

KRAMER. But maybe there's something to it though. They all say the dead one was poisoned. There must be some truth to it.

O'FINN. Not if they're all crazy. And I swear they are. The live ones are the ones who ought to be examined. (*The doorbell rings.*) I'll get it. That's the boys from the morgue. (*He goes to the door, opens it, and admits two white-coated men carrying a stretcher.*) Hello, boys.

FIRST STRETCHER MAN. You got something for us?

O'FINN. Sure have. On the sofa over there.

(*The five ladies immediately arrange themselves as a straight line of mourners, standing downstage of the sofa, between ELIZABETH and the audience. Behind this screen, the two white-coated men put ELIZABETH on the stretcher and carry her out. After the exit of the corpse, the line breaks up, and the ladies follow the stretcher to the door. They alternate between dabbing at their eyes with their handkerchiefs and using their handkerchiefs to wave farewell to ELIZABETH.)*

BIRDIE. Good-bye, dear Elizabeth.

AMANTHA. Good-bye.

NETTIE. Have a good time . . . Oh dear, what am I saying?
(The ladies turn back into the room.)

LUCY. She might be having a good time where she is now. But I doubt it.

AMANTHA. Lucy, you must be more charitable to the dead.

HILDEGARDE. She owed me a week's rent. That's what I just said good-bye to.

BIRDIE. *(Giggling, with a glance at O'FINN)* But, Hildegarde, isn't it worth it?

O'FINN. Well, ladies, we'll get a report from the coroner, and then we'll see if there's anything to this business about poisoning. If there is, we'll be back.

AMANTHA. You mean you're going? You just got here.

O'FINN. There isn't anything for us to do here, ladies. We don't know whether poison was involved. And none of you will answer questions. So we're wasting our time. Come on, Kramer, let's go. *(He starts out.)*

HILDEGARDE. Please, Mr. O'Finn! *(To the other ladies.)* Are we going to let him leave? We've made preparations, you know.

AMANTHA. Oh, yes, the preparations. You can't leave, Mr. O'Finn.

HILDEGARDE. But Mr. O'Finn is quite right. The police do have to work in certain ways. And he doesn't know for sure yet that there's been a murder.

O'FINN. Did you say murder?

HILDEGARDE. Yes, that's what I said.

O'FINN. But even if the lady was poisoned, it could have been suicide or an accident.

NETTIE. *(Giggling)* It wasn't an accident.

O'FINN. Say, you sound like you know it wasn't an accident.

HILDEGARDE. Girls, if we want Mr. O'Finn to stay, we're going to have to give him a little hint.

AMANTHA. Yes, he'll find out anyway after they've examined Eliza-beth. So I think it's quite fair to give him a little hint now.

O'FINN. Okay, okay, you've hooked me. What's the little hint?

AMANTHA. *(After a pause to glance at the others)* Well, there's poison in the house.

O'FINN. There is? What kind? Where?

LUCY. On a shelf in the kitchen. We all know where it is. Rat poison.

KRAMER. Say, O'Finn. There's usually arsenic in rat poison. And remember what they said happened to the dead one? Sounded like arsenic symptoms.

O'FINN. Go get it, Kramer. *(KRAMER exits to the kitchen.)* Well now, we'll soon see about this.

BIRDIE. Yes, we'll see. This gets more exciting all the time. I might swoon at any minute, Mr. O'Finn.

KRAMER. (*Re-enters with a can*) There was rat poison in this can. But the can's empty now.

NETTIE. There, you see. The rat poison is what killed Elizabeth.

O'FINN. Was the can full?

HILDEGARDE. It was about half full yesterday. I remember because I sprinkled some of it in the basement.

O'FINN. Wait a minute now. Let me think. You said the dead lady started acting sick about lunch time. Symptoms from arsenic poisoning begin to show up after about half an hour to an hour. That means she ate or drank something a little bit before lunch. Did she?

HILDEGARDE. It's a strict rule in my house that there's no eating between meals. My boarders get enough for their money as it is. I can't afford to be feeding them between meals.

LUCY. But we all know, Hildegarde, how Elizabeth was about that rule.

NETTIE. Yes, she cheated.

AMANTHA. She'd sneak into the kitchen sometimes, Mr. O'Finn, and get herself an extra cup of tea.

O'FINN. Kramer, go and see if you can find the tea. And see if there's a cup . . .

AMANTHA. Oh, there won't be a cup. She always washed her cup.

O'FINN. Okay, Kramer, just the tea. And we'll take that along with us. If there's arsenic in the tea, we've got a clue.

BIRDIE. Oh, a clue, a clue. Girls, isn't Mr. O'Finn clever?

O'FINN. Ladies, are you trying to make fun of me?

AMANTHA. (*With obvious sincerity*) Oh, dear Mr. O'Finn, we wouldn't make fun of you.

O'FINN. I'm beginning to wonder.

KRAMER. (*Re-enters from kitchen*) Here's the can. There seems to be a white powder mixed in with the tea. We can give it to our chemist to analyze though.

O'FINN. (*Goes to KRAMER and speaks softly*) I'm beginning to think there may be a murder case here after all.

KRAMER. Kind of looks that way, doesn't it?

O'FINN. (*Turning back to the ladies*) All right now, ladies, let's be calm about this thing. Mr. Kramer and I have come to a tentative conclusion—depending on examination of the corpse and the tea, naturally—that a murder was committed here.

BIRDIE. Oh, I'm going to swoon. Mr. O'Finn says there's been a murder.

NETTIE. Don't bother swooning, Birdie. You already knew there was a murder. We *told* Mr. O'Finn, didn't we?

HILDEGARDE. How dare you, Lucy? Mr. O'Finn is a detective. We just gave him a clue, and he figured it out for himself.

NETTIE. Oh, that's all right. Mr. O'Finn, I beg your pardon. You figured it out for yourself.

O'FINN. (*To KRAMER, but loudly*) They're toying with me, Kramer. They're playing games. Hold me back, or I swear by all the saints, there'll be another murder any minute.

BIRDIE. Isn't he cute when he gets mad?

O'FINN. (*Roaring*) Stop it! Stop it! Stop it, I say, or I'll throw you all in the clink!

NETTIE. (*Clapping her hands*) Oh, wouldn't that be fun!

O'FINN. Kramer, this is out-and-out defiance of the law. Call the station and tell 'em to send the paddy wagon. I'll arrest the whole bunch of 'em for obstructing justice.

LUCY. (*Sadly*) Oh, we're going to take a ride, and I let Elizabeth wear my best hat. What on earth will I wear?

KRAMER. (*Goes to O'FINN, and speaks softly*) Losing your temper and threatening won't do a bit of good with this outfit, O'Finn. Now calm down, won't you?

O'FINN. Calm down, is it?

KRAMER. Maybe they're just trying to get your goat.

O'FINN. And they're doing a good job of it. (*Back to the ladies, making a supreme effort to be calm.*) All right now, let's suppose for a moment there was a murder. Who did it? (*There is no reply, but a number of half-suppressed giggles.*) Isn't anybody going to confess?

AMANTHA. Oh, no, Mr. O'Finn, you'll have to find out for yourself.

NETTIE. But you can do it, because you're a detective.

O'FINN. All right, let's put it this way. You all seem pretty certain there was a murder. Do you all know who did it?

BIRDIE. I don't.

NETTIE. Neither do I.

(*The other ladies shake their heads solemnly, but there are also a few more giggles. O'FINN goes to KRAMER again and speaks softly.*)

O'FINN. What do you make of it? Are they holding out on us?

KRAMER. I don't think so. But you never know. I wouldn't put anything past 'em.

O'FINN. Then we've got a funny situation. They all agree there was a murder. They all knew about the poison. And they know one of them did it. But nobody—except the guilty party—knows who.

KRAMER. But they seem anxious for you to find out who did it.

O'FINN. (*Back to the ladies*) Let me ask you all this. You all agreed that Elizabeth was in the habit of breaking the rules and sneaking a cup of tea. Did anybody else ever sneak a cup of tea?

HILDEGARDE. There's no one else that I know of for sure. But I didn't trust any of them.

O'FINN. Then anybody else could have been poisoned.

BIRDIE. Oh, that's right. I never thought of that. And isn't it a good thing we all drank cocoa for lunch, as we always do?

NETTIE. We all had a close call, didn't we?

AMANTHA. Well, it was a chance we simply had to take. But I'm glad it wasn't I who drank the tea. Because then I'd have missed all this.

O'FINN. Hold on now. Hold on a minute. I'm getting a little more of the picture now. Nobody knew there was arsenic in the tea until after Elizabeth started getting sick. But then you all figured out she'd been poisoned. It was just as if you were all *expecting* a murder to happen.

NETTIE. (*Slyly*) You might say we were hoping.

O'FINN. (*Trying not to be distracted by such confusing remarks*) And on top of that, the murderer put arsenic in the tea without knowing who would be the first to drink it. Maybe the odds were on Elizabeth, but the murderer couldn't be sure she'd be the first to drink that tea. As if the murderer wasn't concerned about whom she murdered, but just wanted to commit a murder.

AMANTHA. (*Clapping*) Oh, he's getting warm.

HILDEGARDE. See, I told you he could do it.

LUCY. I think he's as clever as my Herbert was.

AMANTHA. *Your* Herbert? He was never yours that I know of.

LUCY. (*Clasping her heart*) He's always been mine. I hold him right here . . .

O'FINN. Ladies, ladies! Let's stick to the subject, shall we?

HILDEGARDE. Girls, listen to Mr. O'Finn.

O'FINN. Thank you, Miss . . .

HILDEGARDE. Hildegarde.

O'FINN. Yes, Miss Hildegarde. I was saying that the murderer didn't care who she—it had to be a "she," I presume—whom she murdered. That means she didn't have anything particularly against Elizabeth.

NETTIE. But I'm glad it was Elizabeth who drank the tea.

O'FINN. Why are you glad Elizabeth drank the tea?

NETTIE. Because she'd never let anybody else look through the binoculars . . .

(*There is a shocked, embarrassed silence among the ladies. NETTIE understands then the slip she has made. She looks down, blushing. O'FINN senses that there's something important here.*)

O'FINN. What's this about binoculars?

HILDEGARDE. (*Rising and starting to exit*) Oh, I left the kettle on the stove.

O'FINN. Oh, no, you don't. You don't go changing the subject on me like that. What about the binoculars?

HILDEGARDE. (*To NETTIE*) You had to go and give it away. Shame on you.

NETTIE. I'm sorry. (*Starts to cry.*)

AMANTHA. It would have to come out sometime, Hildegarde. Mr. O'Finn is such a clever detective, he'd be sure to find out.

BIRDIE. (*Goes and gets the binoculars, and gives them to O'FINN*) Here they are, Mr. O'Finn.

O'FINN. (*Takes them, but now that he has them, he doesn't know what to do with them. He uses them to look around the room*) Well, what did you look at with this thing?

BIRDIE. (*Giggling*) Don't make us tell you that, dear Mr. O'Finn.

O'FINN. Kramer, have you got any ideas?

KRAMER. Well, you don't use binoculars to look at things inside a house usually. You look at something outside.

O'FINN. Outside? (*He goes to the window and uses the binoculars to look out.*) The only thing I can see is . . . say, you can see my apartment windows from here. . . .

(*There is a veritable gale of giggles. O'FINN turns back, puzzled at first, then angry.*)

HILDEGARDE. Girls, you all must help me in the kitchen now.

(*Embarrassed and looking for an escape, they all run out to the kitchen, still giggling. KRAMER collapses laughing into a chair. O'FINN approaches him.*)

O'FINN. What's so funny?
KRAMER. O'Finn, don't you get it?
O'FINN. No, I don't.
KRAMER. Oh, you're a modest man you are, Dennis O'Finn. You just don't realize what a lady-killer you are.
O'FINN. Cut out the double talk, will you?
KRAMER. (*Rises and stands back to look admiringly at his partner*) Well, why shouldn't you be? Where is there a finer specimen of manhood than an Irish cop? And a bachelor cop at that. And just the right age, too. You have middle-aged dignity. A true man of distinction.
O'FINN. Look, I've had enough teasing for one day. . . .
KRAMER. Oh, but the teasing is just beginning. Can't you see beyond your nose, my darlin' Dennis? The poor old things have nothing to do all day but sit around. And one of 'em has a pair of long-distance specs. So they amuse themselves by spying on everybody within range. And what do they see across the street? The beautiful features and body of O'Finn. They're all in love with you.
O'FINN. Shut up!
KRAMER. But it's a plain fact. They're in love with you. And they say to themselves, wouldn't it be wonderful if we could get a closer look at him? So they ask around, and they find out you're a detective in Homicide. Now, think a minute, Dennis boy, what would you do if you wanted to make a Homicide detective come to your house?
O'FINN. (*The truth dawning*) It's a dirty lie!
KRAMER. You underestimate your charm, Dennis my lad. These ladies are so in love with you that one of 'em committed a murder to get you to come here to investigate it.
O'FINN. (*Stricken*) Oh, no!
KRAMER. Oh, yes! The very fact that they were all delighted with the fact that there was a murder proves it. And the other fact that the murdering lady didn't care who she murdered—just dumped the arsenic willy-nilly into the tea can. They just had to have a murder, that's all. And you're the motive, O'Finn.
O'FINN. (*Grabs KRAMER by the lapels*) You tell this story to anybody in the department, and there'll be another murder. I'll kill you with these bare hands.

17

KRAMER. (*Unafraid*) How does it feel, O'Finn, to be the object of such criminal devotion?

O'FINN. I'll refuse to handle this case, that's what I'll do.

KRAMER. And what excuse will you give the Captain?

O'FINN. (*Crushed, O'FINN lets go of KRAMER*) Oh, the saints preserve me! What will I do?

(*The ladies march in from the kitchen. They're carrying a teapot, cups, saucers, trays of biscuits. etc., all the paraphernalia of a tea party. They're all ecstatically happy.*)

HILDEGARDE. We're having a party, Mr. O'Finn.

AMANTHA. I hope you drink tea, Mr. O'Finn.

LUCY. Don't you worry, Mr. O'Finn, we opened a fresh package of tea. There's no rat poison in this.

BIRDIE. And I baked the biscuits, Mr. O'Finn. There are *two* for you.

LUCY. Yes, Mr. O'Finn can have Elizabeth's biscuit.

HILDEGARDE. (*Hinting*) But there isn't any for Mr. Kramer.

KRAMER. Well, I can take a hint, I guess. Dennis my boy, I just don't have the appeal you have. And I've got to get back to headquarters anyway. And if anybody asks about you, I'll just tell 'em you're here investigating a murder. Ta ta, old chap. And don't drink too much tea. It's terrible strong stuff.

(*KRAMER exits, leaving O'FINN surrounded by the LADIES, who have sat down in a little circle. HILDEGARDE is beginning to pour. Curtain.*)

ACT TWO

(Lights come up on the apron of the stage. O'FINN and KRAMER are there. KRAMER is walking toward O'FINN, as if just entering the room.)

KRAMER. Well, it's official. Just got the word from the Doc. Miss Elizabeth Ellsworth died of arsenic poisoning. There was enough arsenic in her to kill a dinosaur. Say, that's a good comparison, don't you think, O'Finn? Dinosaur. Prehistoric. That's the way you might describe all those old ladies. They're prehistoric.

O'FINN. Don't say that in front of them, Kramer.

KRAMER. Why not?

O'FINN. It would hurt their feelings.

KRAMER. So what?

O'FINN. Well, I don't want to be mean to them. You know something? This may sound kind of funny to you. I realize that one of them seems to have committed a murder, and the rest of them are kind of glad she did. But even so . . . well, they're not really bad old girls.

KRAMER. Just kind of "touched," you mean?

O'FINN. Well sure, but they're kind of sweet. . . .

KRAMER. O'Finn, you sound like their love is being requited.

O'FINN. I didn't say I was in love with 'em.

KRAMER. But you're getting a soft spot in your old Irish heart for 'em. So I suppose when you find out which one of 'em put arsenic flavoring in the tea, I'll have to make the arrest.

O'FINN. When I find out! How am I ever going to find out? Kramer, do you realize what the situation is? The old girls are pretty smart. They committed a murder so a detective would come to their house. So now they're not going to be dumb enough to give the thing away. They want the investigation to go on and on. They don't want it to stop. They're nice as pie to me, but they don't give the slightest co-operation in answering questions or things like that. So I don't have any more idea of who committed the murder than I had when it started.

KRAMER. A dead end, huh?

O'FINN. Absolutely a dead end.

KRAMER. So what are you going to do? Put it in the Unsolved Crime file?

O'FINN. Kramer, I have more pride than that.

KRAMER. Well, you're not going to dump it in my lap.

O'FINN. I didn't say I was. I have a little strategy worked out.

KRAMER. Like what?

O'FINN. The ladies just love to have me there, asking questions and things like that. But they don't give me any sensible answers. They're always changing the subject. Well, so I think the best thing to do is leave 'em alone. Let 'em stew awhile. Maybe then they'll be willing to cough up a clue just to get me back.

KRAMER. O'Finn, you're a genius.

O'FINN. That I may be.

KRAMER. But your strategy better work quick. The Captain will get the report about the arsenic, and then he'll be asking you what the explanation is.

O'FINN. I'll have the answer, Kramer. Right now I think I'll go home and rest my weary bones. The dear girls know where I live. If any of 'em want to spill any beans, they know where to find me.

(The lights go out on the apron. In the black-out the curtain rises, and then the lights come up again on the stage, at 909 Sycamore. Four of the ladies are on stage, and the fifth, MISS HILDEGARDE, is just entering from the kitchen.)

HILDEGARDE. Well, I called up to check, and that reporter will be here any minute.

BIRDIE. Oh, Hildegarde, do you think we're doing the right thing? It seems kind of mean.

HILDEGARDE. Do you know any other way to lure Mr. O'Finn back here?

BIRDIE. No, I suppose not. And it has been rather lonesome without him. It was just yesterday and yet it seems like he's been gone a long time.

AMANTHA. Yes, I miss Mr. O'Finn terribly. This house doesn't seem the same without him. How do you ever suppose we got along without a man around all these years?

LUCY. We didn't. Now I see how empty our lives were.

AMANTHA. But, Lucy, you always said you had Herbert to think about.

LUCY. But I must admit it now. Herbert didn't compare to Mr. O'Finn. *(The doorbell rings.)*

HILDEGARDE. That must be the reporter now.

(She goes to the door and admits the reporter, who to the ladies' surprise, is feminine. JANE ROGERS is in her late twenties, very chic and rather good-looking, a typical career woman sort. She walks into the room and looks around in some amazement.)

JANE. Am I in the right place?

HILDEGARDE. Well, that depends. Who are you?

JANE. Jane Rogers. From the *Herald-Globe*.

HILDEGARDE. You're the reporter?

JANE. That's right. I'm not the regular crime reporter, if that's what you're wondering about. I cover the human interest stuff and the crackpots. Right now I'm working in the crackpot department, I guess you'd say. The editor told me there was somebody who was protesting about lack of police protection.

HILDEGARDE. (*Haughtily*) Well, I don't know what you mean by crackpots, but your information is correct. There's a murderer loose in this house and the police are doing nothing about it.

JANE. (*Doesn't believe it, but plays along. Sits down and takes out a notebook and pencil*) A murderer, huh? Give me the story.

HILDEGARDE. Well, it happened just yesterday. One of my guests, Elizabeth Ellsworth, was poisoned right in this house. Somebody here— one of the ladies in this very room, in fact—put arsenic in the tea, and Elizabeth drank some of it. The police came and took the body away, and asked a few questions. But we haven't heard from them since. So the murderess is still at large.

JANE. (*Still skeptical*) One of you, huh?

AMANTHA. One of us.

JANE. Well, what can I do about it?

HILDEGARDE. You can write an article in your paper. Or an editorial or something. About how the police are neglecting their duty and ought to get on the job.

NETTIE. Because we're all in danger of our lives. Hildegarde bought some more rat poison this morning.

JANE. What's that?

HILDEGARDE. Elizabeth was murdered with rat poison. The police took it away with them yesterday. Of course, it wasn't much good anyway because it was all mixed up with the tea. And we do have some kind of rodents in our basement. So I had to go out this morning and buy some more poison.

JANE. (*Sure of her "crackpot" diagnosis now, but still polite*) So you want the police to protect you because you went out and bought some rat poison. Wouldn't it have been simpler and safer just to go on having the rats?

HILDEGARDE. My dear, how would you like to live under the same roof as a murderess?

NETTIE. Yes, we're scared half to death.

JANE. Why don't you just call the police?

HILDEGARDE. (*Impatient*) We called the police yesterday, and they came. Then they took away the body but left the murderess here, don't you understand? It was Detective O'Finn, if you must know. He knows a murder was committed here yesterday, and he ought to be here today solving it.

NETTIE. I'll bet he's at home right now.

HILDEGARDE. Birdie, get your binoculars and see if he's at home.

BIRDIE. That's a good idea. (*She gets the binoculars, goes to the window, and looks out, much to JANE'S amazement.*)

JANE. (*To HILDEGARDE*) You called her Birdie. Is that short for bird-watcher or what?

HILDEGARDE. She is not watching for birds. She's looking for Detective O'Finn.

BIRDIE. Oh, I see him! I see him!

AMANTHA. What's he doing? Tell us.

BIRDIE. He's in his undershirt. Oh, yes, there's that lovely strawberry mark.

NETTIE. Let me look.

BIRDIE. He's sitting in a chair reading a newspaper. And he's drinking something. (*A little shocked.*) It looks like it might be beer.

AMANTHA. When he should be here drinking tea. And giving us the pleasure of his company.

HILDEGARDE. He's just loafing, that's what he's doing. When he should be protecting us. Birdie, give the binoculars to Miss Rogers. Let her take a look at our fine lazy detective.

JANE. Well, all right, I might as well. (*She takes the binoculars and looks.*) I can't see anybody . . . oh, yes, I do. A man in an undershirt. Is he the one?

BIRDIE. Yes. Do you see the strawberry mark on his left shoulder?

JANE. I suppose that's what it is.

BIRDIE. Isn't he handsome though?

JANE. Well . . . yes . . . oh, oh . . . he's walking over to the window now . . . he's pulled down the shade.

BIRDIE. (*Grabs the binoculars, looks into them, then puts them down*) Girls, that's exactly what he's done. He's pulled down the shade.

NETTIE. That's mean.

HILDEGARDE. It certainly is. He not only won't come over here, but he won't let us look at him. I'll bet he did that on purpose.

JANE. (*Interested finally*) Let me get a few things straight now. You say there was a murder here yesterday?

HILDEGARDE. One of my guests was poisoned. You can verify that with the coroner's office if you like.

JANE. Okay, I'll take your word for it. And you say that man who lives just across the street is the detective who investigated?

AMANTHA. Yes, he was here yesterday for a little while, and he hasn't come back.

HILDEGARDE. And meanwhile we're in fear of our lives.

NETTIE. And besides, we're lonesome.

HILDEGARDE. Nettie, must you forever be saying the wrong thing?

JANE. So you're lonesome, huh?

HILDEGARDE. She meant that we're afraid.

NETTIE. Yes, we're afraid. That's it. Afraid.

JANE. I think I'm beginning to understand. Now look here, girls, you've got to tell me the whole truth, or I won't help you. Are you lonesome or afraid?

BIRDIE. (*After a long pause, during which the LADIES consult one another silently*) We're lonesome.

JANE. And there really was a murder here yesterday?

LUCY. There really was.

JANE. One of you murdered another old . . . I mean, another lady who lived here.

LUCY. That's right. But we're not telling who did it! That's Mr. O'Finn's job.

JANE. Can you tell me this? *Why* was the murder committed?

HILDEGARDE. We can't tell you that.

JANE. I insist.

HILDEGARDE. After all, we've got some pride.

NETTIE. Yes, we're not like the hussies nowadays.

JANE. I think I can put two and two together. A handsome detective lives right across the street from a houseful of old maids . . .

BIRDIE. How dare you!

JANE. Well, you're not married, are you?

BIRDIE. Well, no . . .

JANE. Widows?

LUCY. There was my Herbert . . .

JANE. Your husband?

LUCY. No, he got away.

JANE. Well, let me put it this way. A houseful of spinsters across the street from a handsome detective. A bachelor, I'll bet you. And the spinsters know he's a bachelor. And know he's a detective. And they get together and decide that one of their number is expendable. You know, I think this might make a story after all.

BIRDIE. But we don't want publicity. We want Mr. O'Finn.

HILDEGARDE. Young lady, why don't you threaten Mr. O'Finn? Tell him you'll write a story, showing how he's neglecting his duty.

JANE. Ah, ha, now I understand completely. You all want to *use* me to get O'Finn back here. But that's all right. I think it's a good idea, too. Do you have a phone?

HILDEGARDE. In the kitchen. There.

NETTIE. The number is Lexington 4463.

(*JANE exits to the kitchen.*)

BIRDIE. I don't trust her. She's a hussy.

LUCY. All the young ones are hussies, these days.

HILDEGARDE. But we need her, don't we?

AMANTHA. Why don't we try to listen to what she's saying? (*She crosses and stands with her ear to the kitchen door.*) Oh, the poor man. She's really giving it to him. Telling him it'll be in the morning paper tomorrow. All about a bunch of sweet old ladies being left to the mercy of a fiendish murderess. She says she's interviewing the sweet old ladies right now. And Mr. O'Finn seems to be coming right over. (*She scurries away from the door.*)

JANE. (*Entering from kitchen*) He'll be right over.

BIRDIE. Oh, I must remember to swoon this time. I got so excited yesterday that I completely forgot.

HILDEGARDE. Birdie, control yourself. There's a stranger present.

JANE. Oh, don't let me stand in your way. You girls just go right ahead and drool. I think I understand.

HILDEGARDE. Just what do you mean by that?

JANE. Detective O'Finn is a rather attractive man.

HILDEGARDE. You think so? (*Obviously disturbed.*)

JANE. Oh, yes. The whole situation gets clearer by the minute.

AMANTHA. He had to put his shirt on. Mr. O'Finn is a gentleman, remember.

BIRDIE. I almost wish he'd forget. I'd like to see his strawberry mark up close.

AMANTHA. Birdie, I'm surprised at you.

(*Doorbell rings, and there is a mad rush toward the door.*)

HILDEGARDE. Girls, please! Remember, this is my house, and I'm the hostess. (*She goes to the door, opens it, and admits O'FINN.*)

O'FINN. (*Ignoring HILDEGARDE*) Is Miss Rogers here?

JANE. (*Stepping forward*) I'm Jane Rogers.

O'FINN. Look, Miss Rogers, I'd like to explain a few things.

JANE. You'd better explain. What's the idea, Mr. O'Finn, of leaving these poor, defenseless ladies at the mercy of a killer?

O'FINN. Defenseless? Miss Rogers, one of these ladies *is* the killer.

JANE. Well, of course. But what are you doing to protect the others? The killer may strike again at any time. What are the police doing?

O'FINN. The wheels of justice are turning, Miss Rogers. We've proved conclusively now that Elizabeth Ellsworth died of arsenic poisoning.

NETTIE. But we knew that all the time.

JANE. And what are you doing to find out who the poisoner is?

O'FINN. I'm doing all I can. This is a very peculiar case, you see. . . .

JANE. I've already gathered how peculiar it is. Which brings me to the most important question. Mr. O'Finn, have you established the motivation for the murder?

O'FINN. (*Really embarrassed now*) Motivation? . . . The police have several theories. . . . (*He glances around at the LADIES in desperation.*) Ladies, I'm awfully thirsty. Aren't you serving tea today?

BIRDIE. (*With stern disapproval*) You just had a bottle of beer.

O'FINN. (*Unnerved*) Oh, yes, sure. The binoculars, naturally. But you know something? Beer isn't quite so satisfying any more since I've tasted your tea.

HILDEGARDE. (*Taken in and terribly pleased*) Mr. O'Finn, do you really mean that?

O'FINN. Of course I mean it. Why don't you fix up a pot of the stuff right now?

AMANTHA. And biscuits? I baked some biscuits this morning, hoping you'd come.

O'FINN. I'd love some biscuits.

AMANTHA. You can have *three* today.

O'FINN. That would be great. (*HILDEGARDE and AMANTHA head for the kitchen.*) If the rest of you ladies would help out, it might hurry things up a bit. I tell you, I'm dying of hunger and thirst.

LUCY. Promise you won't go away?

O'FINN. I promise.

BIRDIE. Are you sure you're not just trying to get rid of us?

O'FINN. Now how can you say a thing like that? Let's put it this way. I am anxious for you to go. Because the sooner you go, the sooner you'll be back.

BIRDIE. Oh, Mr. O'Finn, you say the sweetest things. I think I'm going to swoon.

LUCY. Not now, Birdie. You'd only be delaying the tea. Mr. O'Finn has told us how hungry and thirsty he is.

O'FINN. Sure, you don't want me to perish right before your eyes, now do you?

BIRDIE. Oh, heavens no!

O'FINN. Then be off with you. (*BIRDIE, LUCY and NETTIE scurry out to the kitchen.*)

JANE. Mr. O'Finn, you remind me of a bull in a china shop. But you handle these old ladies quite skillfully. Actually you seem fond of them.

O'FINN. I am, in a way. They're nice old ladies.

JANE. Except that one of them committed murder. But the really interesting thing—the thing I imagine our readers would be interested in—is that this murder might be described as a crime of passion.

O'FINN. A crime of passion!

JANE. But of course. What else? It's the most obvious thing in the world that this murder was a crime committed for love. Oh, our readers will eat that up. A variation on the old triangle. What would you call this, a hexagon?

O'FINN. Miss Rogers, are you threatening me?

JANE. I'm merely looking for a story. Let's see, what would the headline be? "Woman Murders Rival for Sake of Detective." Does that appeal to you? Or could I use the word "harem" somewhere?

O'FINN. Harem!

JANE. It's the best word in the dictionary to get over the idea that a group of females is romantically involved with just one male.

O'FINN. And there must be a word for what you're trying to pull off. Libel, maybe.

JANE. Oh, Mr. O'Finn, now you're threatening me. But not frightening me, however. Your charge of libel would make good copy too, you know. Oh, no, Mr. O'Finn, this is too good a story for you to scare me out of.

O'FINN. Well, think of this then as a public-spirited citizen. Do you want to demoralize the police department?

JANE. (*Appraising him admiringly*) Well, I don't know. It might be an interesting project though.

O'FINN. (*Uncomfortable under her gaze*) What are you doing?

JANE. I'm looking at you. I'm trying to decide—if we ran a picture of you for instance—if our readers would believe that you would be capable of arousing such murderous passion in such gentle females. Yes, maybe they would.

O'FINN. (*Embarrassed*) You won't get any picture of me.

JANE. You're not bad, O'Finn. Not bad at all. How's your profile? Oh, very good. Very good. I think you'll do nicely. O'Finn, I can make you the sweetheart of every woman in town. There'll be females of all ages ready to commit murder just to get you to pay attention to them.

O'FINN. (*Pleading*) Miss Rogers, you can't do a thing like this.

JANE. We'll start a wave of homicides. You'll get a spread in *Life*. You'll become a national hero.

O'FINN. Miss Rogers, please, I'll do anything . . .

25

JANE. (*Interested*) Anything? For instance?

O'FINN. Well, anything you say.

JANE. Now, that's interesting. We might talk this over.

O'FINN. That's fine with me.

JANE. But not here. We need the right kind of atmosphere for an important talk like this. Where do you usually go when you take a girl out to dinner?

O'FINN. (*Surprised*) Well, I usually don't take girls out to dinner.

JANE. Oh, I see. A confirmed bachelor.

O'FINN. That's right.

JANE. Well then, maybe it's time you got unconfirmed. Remember, you've got to convince me of something important. (*She walks up close to O'FINN, and stands looking up at him with an obvious invitation. Shy, he doesn't know what to do.*) O'Finn, what is your attraction? You've got a way with women, but just what is your way? Maybe it's your boyish shyness. For instance, I know a lot of men—if they had to convince a girl of something—they might start out by grabbing her and kissing her.

O'FINN. I guess I'm not that type. . . .

JANE. Did you ever think of changing, of trying to be that type?

O'FINN. Miss Rogers, I'm on duty. . . .

(*The ladies enter from the kitchen in a parade, bearing the tea things, which they begin to set up. They seem to be unaware of JANE and O'FINN for the moment.*)

HILDEGARDE. Well, here we are: The tea is steeping. It will be ready in a minute or two.

AMANTHA. And here are the biscuits. One for everybody, and three for Mr. O'Finn.

HILDEGARDE. I still don't see why three. Mr. O'Finn is not a glutton.

AMANTHA. Of course not. But he's a big, strong man who needs lots of food. You're just stingy, Hildegarde.

HILDEGARDE. I'm not stingy. But if you're going to be so extravagant with your baking, I'll have to raise your board, that's all.

NETTIE. Well, this is my own jelly, Hildegarde. My sister sent it for my birthday three years ago.

JANE. (*Interrupting*) Mr. O'Finn, I'm going to telephone my editor. Would you like to come out to the kitchen with me while I talk to him, to make sure I get the facts straight?

O'FINN. (*He understands the threat*) Oh, sure. Excuse us, ladies. We'll be right back.

(*JANE and O'FINN exit to the kitchen. The ladies cease their activities, and stare after them. Silence for a moment.*)

LUCY. Well, did you see that?

HILDEGARDE. That girl's up to something, if you ask me.

NETTIE. What's she up to, do you think?

HILDEGARDE. To no good, that's sure. She has her eye on Mr. O'Finn. Didn't you see how close to him she was standing when we came in? It wasn't ladylike at all.

LUCY. They're all hussies nowadays. I told you that.

AMANTHA. She likes Mr. O'Finn. That's the trouble.

BIRDIE. Well, you can't blame her for that.

AMANTHA. Hildegarde, it's your fault. It was your idea to call a reporter.

HILDEGARDE. But I didn't know it would be a female reporter.

NETTIE. What are we going to do?

AMANTHA. We've got to do something. Mr. O'Finn is supposed to be here investigating our murder. And that hussy is trying to distract him. It's not fair.

BIRDIE. You're right, Amantha. It's not a bit fair. Mr. O'Finn belongs to us.

HILDEGARDE. Mr. O'Finn is much too old for her. She's just a snip of a girl.

AMANTHA. Of course it's natural that she should like him. *We* understand that.

BIRDIE. But he doesn't like her.

HILDEGARDE. I agree with you, Birdie. In fact, I think Mr. O'Finn hates her.

LUCY. But she's pestering him. That's what she's doing. Pestering him.

NETTIE. Well, what can we do about that?

HILDEGARDE. A good question, girls. What can we do about it?

BIRDIE. Let's put our heads together and think real hard.

NETTIE. (*After a long silence*) We could just ask her to leave.

HILDEGARDE. That wouldn't be polite, Nettie.

NETTIE. Do we have to be polite?

HILDEGARDE. Yes. Even if she's a hussy, *we* are ladies.

LUCY. Then I have another idea. I suppose it would be polite.

HILDEGARDE. As long as it's polite. What is your idea, Lucy?

LUCY. We could put some rat poison in her tea.

AMANTHA. What!

LUCY. What I mean is, whoever put the rat poison in Elizabeth's tea could put some in Miss Rogers' tea.

NETTIE. Are you sure that would be polite?

HILDEGARDE. Yes, I think so.

NETTIE. But she's a guest.

HILDEGARDE. So was Elizabeth. A paying guest. But still a guest. Don't be difficult, Nettie. Well, what do you think of the idea?

BIRDIE. She is pestering Mr. O'Finn. We'd be doing him a favor.

AMANTHA. Yes, and I'm sure he'd appreciate it.

HILDEGARDE. And come to think of it, we do need another murder.

NETTIE. Why, Hildegarde?

HILDEGARDE. Well, Mr. O'Finn wasn't paying very much attention to us.

NETTIE. I see. It would remind him of his duty.

AMANTHA. And two murders would be harder to solve than one. So it would take a longer time. And that means he would have to come here oftener. That would be delightful.

NETTIE. And he'd just have to do something about the murder of a reporter.

LUCY. My dears, you overlook the most important reason of all. I agree with Hildegarde that we do need another murder. So if we use Miss Rogers as the victim, it won't have to be one of us.

BIRDIE. That is important, Lucy. I know I don't want to be murdered and miss all the excitement.

NETTIE. But who'll do it?

LUCY. The same person who did it to Elizabeth, silly. Whoever it was.

BIRDIE. Well now, isn't this convenient? The tea is sitting right here, and Miss Rogers is out of the room.

HILDEGARDE. The rat poison is in the kitchen. I'll sneak it out. (*Exits to the kitchen.*)

NETTIE. Oh, isn't this exciting? I feel like an accomplice.

AMANTHA. Are you trying to convince us you're not the poisoner?

NETTIE. Of course I'm not. I couldn't poison anybody. Not even Miss Rogers. I'd like to see her poisoned, but I couldn't do it myself.

LUCY. I wonder who it really is.

BIRDIE. Don't look at me.

LUCY. You needn't play so innocent. (*Teasing.*) We won't tell on you, Birdie.

BIRDIE. But I'm not the one. I wouldn't have the heart to use rat poison to poison a rat.

HILDEGARDE. (*Entering with the rat poison*) I think we'd better take care of that Miss Rogers all right. I don't like her attitude with Mr. O'Finn.

NETTIE. What are they doing in there?

HILDEGARDE. Just talking. But I suspect that isn't Miss Rogers' fault. Mr. O'Finn, however, is a perfect gentleman.

AMANTHA. Well, we'd better hurry up, before they come back. How are we going to arrange it?

LUCY. Yes, that's what I'd like to know. We want to keep who the poisoner is a secret, don't we?

BIRDIE. Oh, yes, it wouldn't be nearly so exciting if it weren't a secret.

AMANTHA. Well then, how are we going to arrange it so that the rest of us won't see the certain one put the poison in Miss Rogers' cup?

BIRDIE. We could all hide our eyes.

LUCY. That's a good idea. But then we might *hear* who it was going over to the tea tray. I can tell your walk, Birdie, from the way your bones creak.

BIRDIE. I don't creak!

LUCY. Yes, you do. Like an old stagecoach.

BIRDIE. Well, I'm not old enough to remember how stagecoaches creak. But maybe you are.

HILDEGARDE. Girls, girls, we haven't time to argue. I have a suggestion. Let's all hide our eyes, like Birdie suggests. But here, I'll put the rat poison on the tray right beside Miss Rogers' cup. Then everybody walk over to the tray, one at a time. And the one who poisoned Elizabeth can put a spoonful of poison into Miss Rogers' cup.

LUCY. That's a good idea. But which one is hers?

HILDEGARDE. This is my good set. But there's a tiny nick in this cup. So we'll give her this one.

AMANTHA. Oh, good, the cup with the nick in it. Now let's hurry, everybody hide their eyes.

(All the LADIES go toward a wall of the room, and turn toward the wall, hiding their eyes.)

BIRDIE. Who's first?

HILDEGARDE. You, Birdie.

BIRDIE. *(Goes to the tray, and stands downstage of it, facing upstage. All the LADIES follow this same procedure. Thus the audience can't see which of the LADIES puts poison in the cup. Then she returns to her original place)* I've finished, and I didn't creak.

LUCY. Oh, yes, you did. Is it all right if I go next? Here I go. *(She repeats the movement.)*

BIRDIE. Talk about creaking!

LUCY. That's the floor, not me. . . . All right, I'm back home.

AMANTHA. I'm going now. Don't anybody peek. Oh heavens, I can't tell one cup from another.

LUCY. If you're going to use the rat poison, at least put it in the right cup.

AMANTHA. I'm not putting it in, but I want to make sure which cup not to drink.

LUCY. Listen to her trying to make out how innocent she is. She's the one I really suspect.

AMANTHA. Well, thank you very much, Lucy.

LUCY. You're welcome.

HILDEGARDE. Hush up, will you? Are you finished, Amantha?

AMANTHA. Yes, I'm finished. I just wanted to make sure which was the right cup, that's all.

NETTIE. It's my turn now. I'm off.

LUCY. What did she say?

BIRDIE. She said she's off.

NETTIE. Oh, I feel so wicked. I feel like Lucrezia Borgia.

BIRDIE. Do you think that means she's putting the poison in?

LUCY. One never knows what Nettie means.

NETTIE. Oh, how I'd like to put some poison in this cup.

LUCY. For heaven's sake, Nettie, if you're not the one who did it before, don't start now. If the cup is too full of rat poison, it may not taste like tea.

NETTIE. You're right, Lucy. I just have to control myself. Well, I'm finished. I'm back now.

HILDEGARDE. That leaves me.

LUCY. Hurry up, Hildegarde.

HILDEGARDE. I'm hurrying. I'm the last one, so I'll take the package of rat poison and hide it.

NETTIE. I'm glad you thought of that, Hildegarde. We wouldn't want to leave it right on the tea tray.

HILDEGARDE. (*She takes the package of rat poison and puts it out of sight*) All right, I'm finished. You can all look now. (*O'FINN and JANE enter.*) Well, we finished just in time.

O'FINN. What did you finish in time?

HILDEGARDE. Fixing the tea, of course. Now if you'll all sit down.

JANE. I don't think I care for any tea. I have to get back to the office right away. Are you coming with me, Dennis?

LUCY. Oh, but you have to drink a cup of tea. We've already poured it.

O'FINN. (*To JANE*) We've got to stay. That's all there is to it.

JANE. Dennis, why do you have to humor these creatures?

O'FINN. (*Gallantly*) I'm not humoring them. I like the tea they serve here, and the biscuits are the finest. If you have to get back to the office, why don't you just go ahead?

JANE. Oh, no, you don't. You're not going to escape that easy. If you're going to stay and drink tea, so am I.

HILDEGARDE. Oh, that's good, Miss Rogers. We're so glad. Now let's everybody sit down. Miss Rogers, you can sit in Elizabeth's place.

JANE. Elizabeth? She was the one who was poisoned, wasn't she?

BIRDIE. Yes, poor Elizabeth.

JANE. If you don't mind, I'd just as soon sit somewhere else.

HILDEGARDE. Please, Miss Rogers. Do sit in Elizabeth's place. Somehow it seems the proper place for you.

JANE. I don't know exactly how to take that remark.

O'FINN. Sure you're not superstitious, are you, Miss Rogers?

JANE. Of course not. (*She sits, but rather uncomfortably*) Say, wasn't it tea which this Elizabeth drank the poison in?

HILDEGARDE. Yes, it was tea. Of course Mr. O'Finn took that batch of tea down to the police station.

JANE. But I remember you said you bought some more rat poison today.

HILDEGARDE. Miss Rogers, would you like to look in the kitchen and see if our new tea has anything unusual in it?

NETTIE. (*Giggling*) We know there isn't any poison in the tea can, don't we?

HILDEGARDE. Nettie, watch yourself. Would you care to investigate, Miss Rogers?

JANE. Oh, no, no, I guess I can drink this tea if everybody else does.

LUCY. That's the spirit, Miss Rogers.

(*JANE takes her cup and lifts it part way to her lips. All the LADIES are silent, frozen, expectant.*)

JANE. Why is everybody looking at me?

HILDEGARDE. We're trying to be polite. Our guest must start drinking before us. You've read the etiquette books, haven't you?

JANE. Oh, of course. (*But she still hesitates.*)

NETTIE. (*Getting flustered*) Oh, I know the trouble. We haven't offered her any sugar. Here, have some sugar. (*She takes the sugar and ladles several spoonfuls into JANE'S cup.*) There now, that'll taste good and sweet.

JANE. I don't take sugar, thank you. (*Looks around at the horrified faces.*) I couldn't possibly drink this stuff now with all that sugar in it.

HILDEGARDE. (*Furious*) Well, Nettie, you've gone and spoiled everything now, haven't you?

O'FINN. (*Soothing*) Nothing's been spoiled at all. Here, I'll take that cup. I like lots of sugar in my tea. (*He exchanges cups with JANE.*)

HILDEGARDE. Oh, no!

NETTIE. Do something, Hildegarde.

HILDEGARDE. Mr. O'Finn, don't drink that tea. I watched you when you were here yesterday, and you didn't use any sugar at all. You don't have to drink that cup.

O'FINN. Now, I know, Miss Hildegarde, how careful you all have to be around here about not wasting anything. So I'm not going to waste this.

LUCY. It needn't go to waste. Nettie likes lots of sugar. Nettie will drink that cup.

NETTIE. I don't think I want any tea today.

LUCY. You drink that cup, Nettie. You put the sugar in.

HILDEGARDE. Here, I'll take it and pour it out and we'll start all over again . . .

O'FINN. I insist on drinking it. (*He starts to drink.*)

HILDEGARDE. Let me have that cup. (*She reaches for it, knocks it out of O'FINN'S hand. The cup shatters on the floor. She is distracted for the moment by this minor tragedy.*) Oh, the cup is broken. And this is my *good* set. Nettie, you'll pay for that cup!

NETTIE. (*Frightened*) I'll pay for it, Hildegarde. I'll pay for it.

(*HILDEGARDE kneels and picks up the pieces.*)

BIRDIE. (*Sympathetic*) But you had to do it, Hildegarde. It was either the cup or Mr. O'Finn. And I think you made the right choice.

LUCY. I don't know about that. A cup in the hand may be worth two detectives in the bush.

AMANTHA. I wouldn't trade a whole set of dishes for Mr. O'Finn's little finger.

HILDEGARDE. (*Rising, still not consoled*) But this was my *good* set.

BIRDIE. But at least that was the cup with the nick in it.

HILDEGARDE. (*Consoled now*) That's right, isn't it? Thank you for reminding me, Birdie. It's not quite so bad when you look at it that way. In that case, I think I'd take Mr. O'Finn.

O'FINN. (*Rising*) Ladies, what is this all about?

JANE. (*Rising*) Dennis, I told you they were all screwy. Now can we go, please? I simply must get back to the office.

HILDEGARDE. (*Sadly*) The tea's cold now anyway.

O'FINN. Then you don't mind, Miss Hildegarde, if we leave? That little accident did kind of spoil the party, I guess.

HILDEGARDE. But the real point, Mr. O'Finn, is when are you going to get around to investigating our murder?

O'FINN. Well, I don't know. There are murders happening every day, you know. . . .

AMANTHA. You're not coming back?

O'FINN. Well, I . . .

HILDEGARDE. Are you going to put that story in the paper, Miss Rogers?

JANE. (*Glancing possessively and triumphantly at O'FINN*) Dennis and I had a little talk about that situation. And we decided that my newspaper shouldn't give the police department any unfavorable publicity. That's our decision *temporarily*. In fact, we were wondering whether there was any murder at all. Oh, of course, there's the fact that a lady died from arsenic poisoning. But there's no *proof* it was murder. Maybe you ladies have just been imagining things. Maybe you're just anxious for a little excitement, and so you'd really like to think it was murder. Probably it was just an accident after all.

O'FINN. Well, we'll be saying good-bye now.

(*O'FINN and JANE go to the door. The LADIES are too stunned and disappointed to protest. O'FINN and JANE exit.*)

AMANTHA. She's got her nerve. An accident indeed!

LUCY. When we all know it was a murder.

BIRDIE. But if Mr. O'Finn thinks it was only an accident, he'll never be back.

HILDEGARDE. That hussy said we can't *prove* it was murder. And she's right. We can't prove it unless one of us would confess. And it's no good confessing, because that would mean the end of Mr. O'Finn's visiting us, too.

AMANTHA. But there must be a way of proving we had a murder in this house.

LUCY. Well, I hate to mention it, but I do sort of have an idea.

BIRDIE. What? Tell us.

LUCY. There's the old saying, you know, that lightning doesn't strike twice in the same place. Nobody could ever believe there could be *two* accidents. So it would have to be two murders.

BIRDIE. You mean somebody else?

LUCY. Yes. Somebody else.

AMANTHA. Could we get Miss Rogers back?

LUCY. I doubt it.

HILDEGARDE. Then that means . . . it will have to be one of us.

(*They all somehow look at NETTIE.*)

NETTIE. I'm never going to drink another cup of tea in my life.

(*Curtain.*)

ACT THREE

(A week later. As the curtain opens, NETTIE is the only one on stage. But NETTIE is dead. She is arranged as on the sofa in the same way ELIZABETH was. To one side is a heap of debris, undisturbed, where a tea tray and its contents have been dropped. As the LADIES come on stage, they walk around this heap.)

AMANTHA. *(Entering)* Nettie dear, this is all I could find. But you always did look good in lavender. *(She puts a lavender handkerchief in NETTIE'S folded hands.)*

LUCY. *(Entering)* I have these earrings that Herbert gave me forty years ago. . . . *(Stops thoughtfully.)* But I wonder . . . maybe I should save them for myself. . . .

AMANTHA. Lucy, you're so morbid.

LUCY. Well, I don't feel too safe around this house these days.

AMANTHA. You could move if you're frightened.

LUCY. That's what you'd like me to do, isn't it? So you who'd be left could have Mr. O'Finn to yourselves. Well, I'm staying. I'll take my chances. *(Attaches the earrings to the corpse.)* Here you are, Nettie. I hope you appreciate this.

BIRDIE. *(Entering)* I really don't have anything to give her. My pearls were all I had. But do you think it would be proper? . . . it isn't very expensive . . . but she liked it. She used to steal it from me sometimes. But besides looking nice, I think Nettie ought to smell nice. *(She douses the corpse with perfume from an atomizer.)*

HILDEGARDE. *(Entering)* Are we all ready? Mr. O'Finn should be here any minute now. Oh, Nettie does look pretty, doesn't she?

LUCY. Best she's looked for twenty years. You know, even though she's dead, she seems to sense that Mr. O'Finn is coming. You see her face? She's smiling.

(A knock is heard at the door. HILDEGARDE rushes to answer it. BIRDIE sprays the room generally. The LADIES form their usual reception line. HILDEGARDE opens the door, and O'FINN and KRAMER enter.)

O'FINN. Well, what is it this time? Or maybe I should say *who* is it?

HILDEGARDE. Our dear Nettie. Nettie Norton. She's dead. Over there on the sofa.

KRAMER. The usual place, huh?

HILDEGARDE. We think they're more comfortable on the sofa. *(O'FINN and KRAMER cross to the corpse, go through the usual motions to determine whether she's really dead.)*

O'FINN. Well, she's dead all right.

LUCY. Of course. We knew that.

KRAMER. (*Taking O'FINN aside*) This is what your strategy led to.

O'FINN. What are you talking about?

KRAMER. They staged one murder to get you here. But you wouldn't stay long enough to please 'em. So now we've got another murder.

O'FINN. But we don't know yet whether it's murder.

KRAMER. Oh, let's don't pretend, Dennis boy. You've been the motivation for another crime. Now what are you going to do about it?

O'FINN. (*Breaks away from KRAMER, takes out notebook, speaks to the LADIES*) Okay, let's have the story. I suppose she was drinking tea. . . .

AMANTHA. Oh, no, we haven't been drinking tea lately. That is, unless we all sit down and drink it together so we can watch the others. We've been too scared.

HILDEGARDE. After all, Mr. O'Finn, you left us here at the mercy of a murderess. No wonder we were scared.

O'FINN. Look here now, don't try to blame this on me. And let me warn you about one thing. Everything's business from here on. We'll have no more tea parties. From now on, we're going to treat you rough.

BIRDIE. Oh, isn't he masterful? We're going to be treated rough. I just can't wait. What are you going to do, Mr. O'Finn?

AMANTHA. I know what I want him to do with me. I want to sit in a chair with a bright light in my eyes and get the third degree.

O'FINN. Stop it! I told you there wasn't going to be any nonsense this time. Now let's get down to business. Who discovered the body?

HILDEGARDE. I did.

O'FINN. Okay, tell me about it.

HILDEGARDE. Well, it was just about time to have our afternoon tea. We were going to drink it together, of course. I was carrying the tray in here from the kitchen, and when I found the body, I was so surprised I dropped the tray. There it is over there. You see, I didn't touch anything. We know how to act now when there's been a murder.

O'FINN. I see that.

HILDEGARDE. I broke all the dishes, too.

O'FINN. I happen to remember, Miss Hildegarde, how valuable your dishes were to you. So you really must have been surprised when you broke all those dishes.

HILDEGARDE. Oh, I was indeed.

O'FINN. But why were you so surprised when you've been telling me all this time that you knew there was a murderer in this house, and you needed police protection?

HILDEGARDE. It isn't every day I stumble across a corpse in my parlor.

O'FINN. No, not every day. But it's been frequent lately. Now where were the rest of you when Miss Hildegarde discovered the body?

BIRDIE. We were all upstairs. I was having my beauty treatment. My mud pack.

LUCY. That old mud pack. It's a waste of time.

BIRDIE. It is not. It's been taking the lines out of my face. I look ten years younger.

LUCY. That still leaves you seventy.

BIRDIE. Hush, Lucy! Mr. O'Finn, she's lying to you about my age. I hope you don't believe her.

O'FINN. I don't know what to believe at this point. Now let's all stick to the subject. You say you were all upstairs . . .

AMANTHA. Yes, we heard Hildegarde's scream and the crash of dishes. I said to myself right then—I'll bet I know what it is. There were Lucy and Birdie across the hall. And it was definitely Hildegarde's scream. So I said to myself—I'll bet Nettie has been murdered. And sure enough.

O'FINN. Naturally you all ran downstairs.

AMANTHA. Oh, yes. Nettie was lying right beside the sofa. So it wasn't hard to pick her up and put her where she'd be more comfortable.

O'FINN. And you kind of dressed her up. Like you did the other one.

KRAMER. Sure, O'Finn. For you, naturally.

O'FINN. Kramer, can't you find anything to do besides making smart remarks? Why don't you pick up those broken dishes?

KRAMER. Okay, okay. (*He starts picking up the broken dishes. He takes them to one side, and from here on, till he speaks again, he concentrates on the dishes, starting to piece them together.*)

BIRDIE. How do you like the perfume Nettie is wearing?

O'FINN. (*Understanding*) You mean you put perfume on her after . . . ?

BIRDIE. Well, it was her last chance. And this is quite an occasion for her. . . . .

(*There is a knock on the door. O'FINN goes to answer it.*)

O'FINN. That'll be the stretcher boys. (*Opens the door.*) Come in, lads. You'll find the merchandise right where it was the last time.

FIRST STRETCHER MAN. You mean you got another one?

SECOND STRETCHER MAN. What's going on here, O'Finn? This is getting to be our regular Tuesday stop.

O'FINN. Cut the comedy. Just pick up the stiff, will you.

(*The STRETCHER MEN go to pick up the body. As before, the LADIES line up downstage of the sofa, facing upstage, masking the removal of the body from the audience. The MEN then carry their burden out the door. The LADIES follow, waving good-bye.*)

BIRDIE. Good-bye, Nettie. Take care of yourself.

LUCY. (*Back to the other LADIES*) She was still smiling. I don't think she minded at all.

AMANTHA. Nettie was always a good sport.

(*As the two STRETCHER MEN exit, JOHNSON, the police fingerprint technician, enters.*)

JOHNSON. Hi, O'Finn. Anything for me to do?

O'FINN. Hello, Johnson. Just hang around a minute, will you? Now, ladies, a couple more questions. Whenever there's been a murder in this house, you all seem to know quite a few details about it before the police do. Now tell me, how do you think she was murdered?

AMANTHA. Oh, she was poisoned. How else?

O'FINN. What makes you think that?

HILDEGARDE. You took away our rat poison, Mr. O'Finn, but I had to buy some more. So it was probably arsenic again.

O'FINN. But you said you didn't drink tea any more. . . .

HILDEGARDE. Oh, I don't think it was the tea this time. In fact, Nettie was more afraid than anybody else. So she didn't drink tea at all. Not even when we were all together.

O'FINN. What did she drink?

LUCY. Buttermilk.

O'FINN. Johnson, go out in the kitchen and see if you can pick up any clear prints on any buttermilk bottles or on that package of rat poison.

JOHNSON. Buttermilk and rat poison. Coming right up. (*Exits to kitchen.*)

O'FINN. I have no doubt she was poisoned. And the prints will probably prove who did it. Now does the guilty party want to confess and save us some trouble? (*A silence.*) Okay, I should have known you wouldn't. Then can anybody give me any information which would lead to solving the murder? (*Another silence.*) Okay, I see it's going to be just like last time. Well, let me remind you of something. You said there was a murderer in this house. You said you're all frightened. We've seen the killer strike a second time. Don't you realize the danger you're in? If you hold back information, you may be letting the killer remain free that much longer. Maybe just long enough to strike a third time.

BIRDIE. Mr. O'Finn is right. We're all in danger.

AMANTHA. Do you have any clues, Birdie?

BIRDIE. I wish I did. But I don't.

O'FINN. Can't anybody tell me anything? (*A silence.*) All right, you asked for it. I'll tell you something. The Captain down at headquarters is going to find it very strange that there have been two murders in the same house. And if they're not solved he's going to blame me. He'll have me back in uniform pounding a beat. And with these feet of mine not what they used to be at all. So you see, ladies, this is pretty important to me. It means my job. I've got to find out who's been spiking the tea and the buttermilk around here. So I'm not going to leave this place until I do.

BIRDIE. (*After a moment to let it sink in, she claps her hands*) Oh, wonderful! Mr. O'Finn is going to stay.

AMANTHA. He's going to live here!

LUCY. Do you think that's quite proper, though? We've always had just lady boarders.

HILDEGARDE. It's up to me to say what's proper in this house.

BIRDIE. Oh, please let him stay, Hildegarde. There are two rooms vacant now, Elizabeth's and Nettie's. He could have his choice.

AMANTHA. Oh, just imagine. Mr. O'Finn for breakfast and dinner every day. And on his days off, for tea besides.

O'FINN. Ladies, please . . .

HILDEGARDE. But he'd have to pay board and room just like everybody else. In fact, he'd have to pay twice as much. He'd eat twice as much as any of us, you know.

AMANTHA. Oh, Hildegarde, you're so mercenary.

HILDEGARDE. I have to be. I've lost two boarders, remember. And I didn't invite you people into my house because I like your company.

BIRDIE. Well, if Mr. O'Finn can't pay his board, we'll all chip in. . . .

O'FINN. Ladies, stop it! Let me get a word in. I didn't say I was going to move in.

KRAMER. Say, you know something, O'Finn. There's one thing sure. If you moved in, there wouldn't be any more murders here. There wouldn't have to be.

O'FINN. Well, once and for all, I'm not moving in! I just said I was going to stay here till I solved these two murders.

LUCY. (*Slyly*) But, Mr. O'Finn, that may take a long time. You haven't found any clues at all yet.

O'FINN. Don't worry, I'll find some. (*Shouting toward the kitchen.*) Hey, Johnson, are you through in there?

JOHNSON. (*Entering*) Got a few prints, O'Finn. Can't tell right off whether they belong to just one person or to more than one. But I do have some prints.

O'FINN. All right. Then I want you to take the prints of all these ladies here.

BIRDIE. (*Ecstatic*) We're going to have our fingerprints taken!

JOHNSON. (*He sets up his apparatus, ink pad and sheets of paper, in a corner*) All right, ladies, who's first?

BIRDIE. Me. Me. I'm first. (*Goes to JOHNSON, and he takes her hand.*) How dare you, young man? What do you think you're doing?

JOHNSON. Lady, I have to do this. I have to take each finger, and ink it, and then roll it on the paper to make sure we get a complete print.

BIRDIE. Can't I do it myself?

JOHNSON. We've got to make sure it's done right.

BIRDIE. But, young man, you're holding my hand.

JOHNSON. Lady, don't worry. That's as far as I'm going to go. I promise not to squeeze it.

LUCY. You ought to be glad, Birdie. How long has it been since a man held your hand?

BIRDIE. Never you mind how long it's been. . . . By the way, Mr. O'Finn, do you know how to take fingerprints?

KRAMER. Sure he does. In fact, he's very good at it. Dennis, why don't you take the ladies' fingerprints? That's what they're hinting.

O'FINN. Kramer, you keep out of this.

AMANTHA. Oh, please, Mr. O'Finn. We'd much rather have you do it.

BIRDIE. Mr. O'Finn, this man has gotten my fingers all black.

O'FINN. It can be washed. All right, who's next? Miss Amantha, it's your turn.

AMANTHA. (*Obeying*) Mr. O'Finn, you're just being stubborn.

O'FINN. That's right. I'm a stubborn man.

LUCY. That's not stubbornness. It's strength of character. My Herbert had strength of character.

HILDEGARDE. Lucy, I can't understand why you still admire Herbert. Strength of character, indeed. He left you, didn't he?

LUCY. That's right. He got away. I was the stubborn one. The way I chased that man. And the way he resisted me. That was real strength of character.

O'FINN. Ladies, let's get down to business. We'll analyze the buttermilk at the lab to make sure whether there was arsenic in it. And, of course, we'll make sure what Miss Nettie died of. But meanwhile, I think we can assume it was arsenic poisoning, and the arsenic was in the buttermilk. Now did anybody else besides Nettie drink buttermilk?

HILDEGARDE. Nobody else. It wasn't furnished with the regular board. She always bought it herself at the grocery store.

O'FINN. Then the murderer knew who was going to be murdered.

LUCY. Must have. But it was Nettie's own fault. She should have known better than to drink buttermilk. It's awfully easy to put a white powder like rat poison into buttermilk.

AMANTHA. But poor Nettie wasn't very bright. It's your turn to be fingerprinted, Lucy.

LUCY. (*Going to JOHNSON*) Now see here, young man, I don't want to get my hands soiled.

JOHNSON. There's no other way of doing it, ma'am.

O'FINN. Miss Lucy, please cooperate.

LUCY. Well, all right, Mr. O'Finn, if *you* say so.

O'FINN. Now let's continue. So the murderer knew that it would be Miss Nettie who would be poisoned when she put the rat poison in the buttermilk. But why did she want to poison Miss Nettie?

KRAMER. (*Looking up from his work*) O'Finn, you're going around in circles. You know the answer to that question. And you'll get nowhere asking it. We know the motive, man. And there's no use pretending that there's any other motive.

O'FINN. Shut up, Kramer.

KRAMER. I won't shut up. It's obvious to me that Miss Nettie was killed for only one reason. There had to be another murder, to get you back into the house, O'Finn. And Miss Nettie was a handy victim simply because it's so easy to slip rat poison into something like buttermilk.

BIRDIE. Oh, that's very clever.

HILDEGARDE. (*Angrily*) But Mr. O'Finn should have thought of it.

KRAMER. Mr. O'Finn would have thought of it, except that he's trying to pretend to himself that these murders have been happening for a different reason than the real reason. O'Finn, my boy, you're in a spot.

O'FINN. I'm not denying that.

KRAMER. I can see it all now. Here we have two murders that can't be solved. We know the motivation, but the same motivation applies to all the suspects. So you know what's going to happen? We'll keep on having murders. Three more murders. Till we're down to just one of you ladies left alive. And then we'll have the guilty one. O'Finn, that's the only way to solve this case.

BIRDIE. Oh, dear!

KRAMER. That's the way it is, ladies. The great O'Finn is stumped.

BIRDIE. Mr. O'Finn, we were all thinking you were a smart detective.

AMANTHA. I'd give you a hint, Mr. O'Finn, if I had one.

BIRDIE. And I'd confess if I had anything to confess.

O'FINN. (*Furious*) Look, I don't want pity from any of you. Let's get on with the fingerprinting. Miss Hildegarde, it's your turn. And do be quiet, Kramer. Police work is scientific these days. Science will lick this problem.

KRAMER. Science will never lick these ladies, O'Finn. (*Goes back to piecing dishes together.*)

HILDEGARDE. Come on now, Mr. O'Finn, think hard. We're all on your side. . . . (*To JOHNSON.*) Young man, watch what you're doing, please. You pinched me.

JOHNSON. Beg your pardon, ma'am. But you've got to hold still.

KRAMER. Hey, O'Finn, come here a minute. Here's something that's kind of funny.

O'FINN. (*Going over to KRAMER*) What's on your mind?

KRAMER. I've been playing around with these broken dishes. Remember the landlady said she was coming in with the tea tray when she discovered the body. And she said she was so surprised that she dropped everything. Well, I've been piecing all these dishes together. Just out of curiosity, kind of. And there's a funny thing. I can't find handles for any of the cups.

O'FINN. No handles?

KRAMER. Not a one.

O'FINN. Do you think it means anything?

KRAMER. How do I know? You're the smart detective. Maybe it's a clue and maybe it isn't.

O'FINN. Well, if it's a clue, it's the first one. I guess we shouldn't be proud. (*Back to the LADIES.*) Ladies, Mr. Kramer has discovered an odd thing. He's been examining the dishes that Miss Hildegarde dropped and broke. He's been trying to put them back together. And there are no handles for the cups.

BIRDIE. Is that a clue, Mr. O'Finn?

O'FINN. I don't know. But now Miss Hildegarde said she didn't touch anything. She left everything as it was for the police. Now what about the rest of you? Did anybody else touch those broken dishes?

BIRDIE. Certainly not.

AMANTHA. Not me.

LUCY. Why should we touch the broken dishes?

O'FINN. That's what I'm going to find out. Who meddled with the broken dishes. Why they did it. And where are the missing cup handles.

BIRDIE. Oh, we do have a clue. This is exciting.

AMANTHA. Mr. O'Finn, we'll all help you look.

O'FINN. No, you don't. We'll do our own looking.

(There is a knock at the door. HILDEGARDE opens the door, and JANE ROGERS enters.)

JANE. Dennis, I was down at your precinct looking for you, and the desk sergeant said you were at 909 Sycamore. *(She looks around at the LADIES, counting them.)* Oh, there are only four left. Has there been another murder?

O'FINN. Brilliant deduction. There's been another murder, all right.

JANE. Which one this time? Oh, it doesn't matter. They were all alike.

HILDEGARDE. Now see here, you young hussy . . .

JANE. Take it easy, grandma.

HILDEGARDE. I am not a grandmother.

JANE. Oh, that's right. You never got a husband, did you?

O'FINN. Jane, be quiet. You needn't be so nasty with these ladies.

JANE. Still defending them, Dennis? Even after another murder?

O'FINN. I just don't like you to be insulting them, that's all.

JANE. Because they're somebody's mothers? They're just a bunch of old maids.

O'FINN. Jane, I'm warning you.

JANE. I'm warning you, Dennis dear. Now why, I wonder, was there another murder? I think I can guess. We told them, didn't we, that the first homicide was probably an accident? And then you said you were going to stay away from the house. Because maybe it had been an accident, and the ladies were just dramatizing it so they could have the company of the big handsome policeman. But then your little scheme of ignoring them backfired, didn't it? They didn't want to be ignored. So they committed another murder to make you come back. My, my, the behind-the-scenes story possibilities of this get better all the time.

O'FINN. Jane, we've already discussed this.

JANE. Yes, we've discussed this, but not very satisfactorily. And besides, the story gets better all the time.

JOHNSON. Say, O'Finn, I've got all the prints, haven't I? Can I go now?

O'FINN. Sure, go ahead. Get me the results as quick as you can.

(JOHNSON exits out the front door.)

JANE. So we're taking fingerprints now. Getting very scientific. I presume that you haven't solved the case yet.

O'FINN. No, I haven't solved it.

JANE. More and more interesting. Now I wonder how you're going to keep this out of my paper. It's a story that's crying to be printed.

O'FINN. Jane, we agreed . . .

JANE. It wasn't a very satisfactory agreement. And after we agreed, ou stood me up twice in one week. But anyway, now that the story has gotten better, the price of silence is going up.

O'FINN. How can you do this to me? You know how they'd take this story in the department. I'd be ruined.

JANE. So you've got to solve two problems. Who killed the old ladies. And how to keep the motivation for the murders quiet.

O'FINN. I'm working on the first problem, can't you see? And you're interrupting me. And we'll have to discuss the second problem in private.

JANE. You're just stalling. Like you did the last time. The story's hot. It can't wait.

O'FINN. (*Desperately*) Come on in the kitchen a minute, will you?

JANE. Just you and me? How exciting. Of course I'll go out in the kitchen.

(*O'FINN and JANE exit to the kitchen.*)

HILDEGARDE. Well, I'd like to know what's going on. Right in my own kitchen, too.

KRAMER. You mean you don't know?

HILDEGARDE. If I knew, I wouldn't be asking.

KRAMER. Well, maybe you ought to know. Though I doubt if you'd understand. For one thing, this is all your fault. You ladies are the ones responsible for that dame getting in on this. You had to call a reporter.

HILDEGARDE. But we didn't know the reporter was going to be a . . . a dame.

KRAMER. Okay, but that's the way it happened. And of all dames it had to be, this Jane Rogers is the worst. She's an old maid too—if you'll pardon the expression. And my boy Dennis O'Finn seems to have some kind of special attraction for old maids. Whatever it is, I guess she fell for him for the same reason you all did.

HILDEGARDE. We did not *fall* for him.

KRAMER. Don't play innocent now. One of you four committed two murders—two murders, no less—just to get our hero in here to investigate. Well, Jane Rogers fell, too. And she threatened to print the real story of O'Finn's fatal charm. It was a good story, and she wanted to write it. But then she started liking O'Finn better than the story. So she told O'Finn that she might *not* print the story if he'd . . . do certain things . . .

AMANTHA. What things?

BIRDIE. Oh, don't be so dense, Amantha. I may be the oldest one here, but I'm not so old that I don't remember what things.

KRAMER. Anyway, she's given O'Finn a merry chase this past week. He did his best to stall her off. He made dates with her, and didn't keep them. That's why he's in hot water with her now. And every time you gals commit a murder, the water gets hotter.

HILDEGARDE. Are we to understand Mr. O'Finn doesn't care for this Jane Rogers . . . dame?

KRAMER. You guessed it. Now understand, it's not that Dennis doesn't care for the fairer sex. He does, but no single one in particular. He likes to spread his charms around. That's why he's gone through life as a bachelor.

LUCY. And Miss Rogers is chasing him, isn't she? Oh, I can tell. I

41

chased my Herbert for years, so I know how it's done. And Mr. O'Finn doesn't want to be caught any more than Herbert did.

KRAMER. He is caught though. The Rogers dame has the goods on him. She can print a story that can kill him. What's he going to do?

HILDEGARDE. If he can't do anything himself, we've got to help him.

(*O'FINN and JANE enter from the kitchen.*)

JANE. Folks, hold on to your seats. We've got something to tell you.

KRAMER. (*Worried*) What is it, O'Finn?

O'FINN. Jane will tell it.

JANE. (*Having fun*) I think the girls will appreciate this. Sit down, girls, sit down. This will shock you a bit. (*The LADIES, confused, sit down.*) I know how fond of Dennis you all were. All of you. And of course one of you really went overboard for him. Whichever one of you has been playing with the arsenic, I mean. And I really am grateful to you too, by the way. You're the ones who arranged for me to meet Dennis. Well, I'll tell you what's happened. Dennis and I are engaged.

BIRDIE. (*Rises, then begins to totter*) Oh, no, I don't believe it. . . . Mr. O'Finn belongs to us. . . . Say it isn't so, Mr. O'Finn . . .

O'FINN. (*Sadly*) I'm afraid it's true.

BIRDIE. Oh dear . . . oh dear . . . what will we do . . . you'll be moving away, I suppose . . . that snug little apartment of yours won't be big enough for two. . . .

O'FINN. (*Miserably*) I guess not.

BIRDIE. Oh, I can't stand it. . . . I'm going to swoon. . . . (*And this time she does.*)

O'FINN. (*Rushes to catch her*) Miss Birdie! Kramer, get a glass of water from the kitchen. (*KRAMER goes.*) Now why did you have to upset 'em like this, Jane?

JANE. I can brag if I want to. I don't see why you have to worry about these creatures.

O'FINN. Don't call 'em creatures! This one here's an old sweetheart, she is.

BIRDIE. (*Opening her eyes*) What did you say? Sweetheart?

KRAMER. (*Entering from kitchen*) Here's a glass of water. (*Hands it to O'FINN.*)

O'FINN. (*Gives BIRDIE the water and eases her back down to her chair*) Now you just drink this, Miss Birdie, and you'll feel a lot better.

BIRDIE. Did you say sweetheart? Oh, I'm going to swoon again.

O'FINN. Now, now, Miss Birdie. You don't need to do that. Just have a drink of water, and then sit there and rest.

BIRDIE. (*To the other ladies*) Did you hear that? He called me sweetheart.

AMANTHA. (*Obviously jealous*) He said you were *a* sweetheart. Not *his* sweetheart.

O'FINN. (*Gallantly*) But I meant *my* sweetheart. In fact, you're all my sweethearts.

42

JANE. Oh, for heaven's sake! Dennis O'Finn, you're acting like an idiot. Come on with me. Let's get out of this nut house.

HILDEGARDE. Mr. O'Finn is on duty, investigating a murder. And he's got to stay in this nut house till he finishes.

O'FINN. That's right, Jane. I can't leave my job.

JANE. Your job! O'Finn, I'm not marrying you for your brilliant detective work. These old ladies have pulled the wool over your eyes from the beginning. You don't have the faintest idea who the murderer is. You don't have a single clue.

O'FINN. (*His pride hurt*) I'll have you know we've uncovered a very important clue. These cups I'm talking about. Miss Hildegarde was carrying a tray in from the kitchen when she discovered the body. She dropped the tray in her surprise and broke everything. But Kramer has been putting the pieces together, and we can't find handles for any of the cups.

JANE. And do you seriously call that a clue?

O'FINN. Of course.

JANE. Well then, what does it mean?

O'FINN. (*Stumped*) We don't know exactly what it means yet.

JANE. For pity's sake, Dennis! What's the clue worth if you don't know what it means? Believe me, this kind of detective work is not for you. If you think you've got a clue there, you're dumber than I think.

HILDEGARDE. If you think he's so dumb, why do you want to marry him?

JANE. Listen here, grandma, that's my business.

HILDEGARDE. Mr. O'Finn is not dumb. All of us here have perfect confidence in him. We know he'll find the murderer.

JANE. Well, you may have confidence in him, but I don't. If I lived in this house, I wouldn't eat or drink a thing here.

LUCY. Dearie, if I were you I wouldn't either.

O'FINN. Girls, please . . .

HILDEGARDE. Mr. O'Finn, those cup handles *are* a clue. You just go right ahead and show that . . . that dame . . . how smart you are.

O'FINN. Okay, okay. But will you all shut up a minute and give me a chance to think!

AMANTHA. Yes, be quiet, everyone. Mr. O'Finn is thinking.

JANE. (*After a silence*) I can hear the rusty wheels going around.

LUCY. (*To JANE*) Miss Rogers, while Mr. O'Finn is thinking, would you like a cup of tea?

BIRDIE. (*After another silence*) Oh, Hildegarde, isn't it a good thing that those broken dishes weren't your good set?

AMANTHA. Yes, that would have been a shame if you'd broken your best dishes.

O'FINN. Wait a minute. What's all this you're talking about?

AMANTHA. Those weren't the good dishes. Hildegarde saves the good dishes for when we have company. But she's got lots of those old ones.

BIRDIE. Oh, yes, lots of extra ones now. Especially when there used to be six of us, and now there are only four.

O'FINN. The old dishes, is it? (*He goes over and examines them.*)

And lots of **extra** ones. And broken cups with no handles . . . or is it cups with no handles? Kramer, I think we've got something here.

BIRDIE. Tell *us*, Mr. O'Finn.

O'FINN. Well, this is the way I think it happened. The lady who brought this tray of dishes in, and then dropped 'em and broke 'em, is a frugal, hard-working soul who for years has managed to support herself by running this boarding house. She has had to learn to save and scrimp and be very careful of her meager possessions. That's why the cups are without handles. She picked out cups whose handles were already broken. Because she knew *in advance* she'd be dropping the tray and breaking 'em. Because she knew there'd be a corpse in this room even *before* she entered. So what, she asked herself, was the sense of breaking her best dishes?

HILDEGARDE. Oh, that's clever of you, Mr. O'Finn. That's exactly what I thought.

O'FINN. Miss Hildegarde, I arrest you for the murders of Elizabeth Ellsworth and Nettie Norton.

LUCY. Was it really you, Hildegarde?

HILDEGARDE. (*Proudly*) It was really me.

BIRDIE. And here I thought all the time it was you, Lucy.

LUCY. And I suspected Amantha.

AMANTHA. And I'd have picked Birdie.

BIRDIE. Isn't that amazing? Nobody thought it was Hildegarde. Hildegarde, we must congratulate you. You were very clever.

HILDEGARDE. But not clever enough to fool Mr. O'Finn. It's Mr. O'Finn who ought to be congratulated.

AMANTHA. Oh, yes, by all means. Mr. O'Finn, you were simply marvelous.

LUCY. You see how wrong you were, Miss Rogers. Mr. O'Finn is a very clever detective.

HILDEGARDE. Yes, Miss Rogers. I think you'd better take back those nasty things you said about him.

JANE. Grandma, I just don't understand this whole thing, I guess. He just arrested you for murder, and you're congratulating him. You seem happy!

HILDEGARDE. Well, of course. I'd have been very disappointed in Mr. O'Finn if he hadn't figured it out. I expected him to arrest me. After all, I did poison Elizabeth and Nettie, didn't I? I know that wasn't very nice. So I expected to be arrested.

O'FINN. (*Gently*) I'm very sorry, Miss Hildegarde, but I'm glad you understand. You'll have to come along now.

HILDEGARDE. (*Coquettishly*) With you, Mr. O'Finn?

O'FINN. With me.

HILDEGARDE. Oh, how wonderful.

BIRDIE. Hildegarde, you're the lucky one.

AMANTHA. We envy you, Hildegarde.

JANE. Dennis, can't your friend Kramer take the old lady to jail? You and I have something else to do, remember?

HILDEGARDE. I stand on my rights as a citizen. I insist that Mr. O'Finn be my escort.

O'FINN. I'll be your escort, Miss Hildegarde.

HILDEGARDE. Thank you. May I go and get my hat, please?

O'FINN. Sure. Go get your hat. It's a sunny day, and you don't want to be getting freckles and ruining your complexion. (*HILDEGARDE exits to kitchen, blushing and giggling.*) Well, Kramer, that wraps it up. I'm relieved, I tell you that.

JANE. I'm glad too, Dennis. Now you can give all your attention to me.

HILDEGARDE. (*Entering with a hat on and carrying a fancily wrapped box of candy*) Well, here I am, ready to go. And, Miss Rogers . . . I may not be around at the time of the ceremony, so here's a little wedding present ahead of time.

JANE. A box of candy . . . well, thanks . . .

O'FINN. That's awfully nice of you, Miss Hildegarde. . . .

HILDEGARDE. I want you to promise me one thing, Dennis. Will you promise?

O'FINN. Sure I promise.

HILDEGARDE. I absolutely forbid you to eat any of that candy in that box. I want Miss Rogers to eat every bit of it. . . . Come along now . . . off to jail!

(She starts toward the door as the lights go out. In the black-out, the curtain descends, and the lights come up on the apron. O'Finn is already standing in the light. If the audience should be applauding, he silences them and speaks directly to them.)

O'FINN. Now wasn't that a funny thing? I never guessed that there was arsenic in that candy till I read the obituaries. I was kind of sorry for Jane, but I was glad though that I didn't have to marry her. It solved one of my problems, but I still had another one. You see, I didn't trust those three old ladies who were left. They'd had such a lot of fun with those murders, one of them might try it again. So I did the proper thing. I didn't want any more murders on my conscience. So I transferred to the Arson Squad. You know what that is, checking on fires and such. And I made it a point to tell Miss Lucy and Miss Amantha and Miss Birdie that I wouldn't be in Homicide any more. I'd be in Arson.

(There is a sound of a siren from backstage and KRAMER breaks through the curtains.)

KRAMER. Hey, O'Finn, there's a fire you should be investigating. Address is 909 Sycamore Street. A boarding house for old ladies.

(Black-out.)

OTHER TITLES AVAILABLE FROM SAMUEL FRENCH

COCKEYED
William Missouri Downs

Comedy / 3m, 1f / Unit Set

Phil, an average nice guy, is madly in love with the beautiful Sophia. The only problem is that she's unaware of his existence. He tries to introduce himself but she looks right through him. When Phil discovers Sophia has a glass eye, he thinks that might be the problem, but soon realizes that she really can't see him. Perhaps he is caught in a philosophical hyperspace or dualistic reality or perhaps beautiful women are just unaware of nice guys. Armed only with a B.A. in philosophy, Phil sets out to prove his existence and win Sophia's heart. This fast moving farce is the winner of the HotCity Theatre's GreenHouse New Play Festival. The St. Louis Post-Dispatch called Cockeyed a clever romantic comedy, Talkin' Broadway called it "hilarious," while Playback Magazine said that it was "fresh and invigorating."

Winner!
of the HotCity Theatre GreenHouse New Play Festival

"Rocking with laughter...hilarious...polished and engaging work draws heavily on the age-old conventions of farce: improbable situations, exaggerated characters, amazing coincidences, absurd misunderstandings, people hiding in closets and barely missing each other as they run in and out of doors...full of comic momentum as Cockeyed hurtles toward its conclusion."
–Talkin' Broadway

OTHER TITLES AVAILABLE FROM SAMUEL FRENCH

MURDER AMONG FRIENDS
Bob Barry

Comedy Thriller / 4m, 2f / Interior

Take an aging, exceedingly vain actor; his very rich wife; a double dealing, double loving agent, plunk them down in an elegant New York duplex and add dialogue crackling with wit and laughs, and you have the basic elements for an evening of pure, sophisticated entertainment. Angela, the wife and Ted, the agent, are lovers and plan to murder Palmer, the actor, during a contrived robbery on New Year's Eve. But actor and agent are also lovers and have an identical plan to do in the wife. A murder occurs, but not one of the planned ones.

"Clever, amusing, and very surprising."
– *New York Times*

"A slick, sophisticated show that is modern and very funny."
– WABC TV

OTHER TITLES AVAILABLE FROM SAMUEL FRENCH

THE RIVERS AND RAVINES
Heather McDonald

Drama / 9m, 5f / Unit Set

Originally produced to acclaim by Washington D.C.'s famed Arena Stage. This is an engrossing political drama about the contemporary farm crisis in America and its effect on rural communities.

"A haunting and emotionally draining play. A community of farmers and ranchers in a small Colorado town disintegrates under the weight of failure and thwarted ambitions. Most of the farmers, their spouses, children, clergyman, banker and greasy spoon proprietress survive, but it is survival without triumph. This is an *Our Town* for the 80's."
– *The Washington Post*